Living in the Shadow of Death

LIFE AFTER DEATH DAY
BOOK 1

DONNA AUGUSTINE

Chapter One

DEATH DAY

The end of the world didn't come the way I expected. I wasn't sure anyone could've predicted how it went down. People were busy working. Children played at the park, shrieking in delight as they chased each other around the playground. The sun was shining and there wasn't a single gray cloud to foreshadow what was about to befall us. There was no warning at all, no time to prepare, no indication that in a matter of minutes, the entire world would devolve into a chaos of unimaginable scope.

My biggest worry that day had been getting something to eat after my shift at the roller rink. I'd only been living with my father on Staten Island for three months. After my mother finally succumbed to cancer, I didn't have a dime left to do anything but crawl back here and crash on his couch.

I parked my twenty-year-old Jeep on the street, and a horde

of kids came biking down the sidewalk. I dodged the onslaught and made it into my favorite pizza place.

Pete, the son of the owner, smiled and plated up a slice. He slid it across the counter toward me.

"Pip, me and my roommates are having a party tonight. Want to come?" His shaggy locks nearly covered one eye as his boyish grin highlighted a single dimple.

This was the tenth or twelfth invite Pete had extended without progress, and yet he still offered it up with optimism. The whole situation might've been a bit awkward if he hadn't been so pleasant after each rejection. He treated his invites like he'd entered some sort of cross-country marathon and was determined to stay the course.

Maybe I should've found a different pizza place, but it was hard to make the move until he soured on me. They made a thin slice that was unlike anything else in the area. If there was one thing that made moving to New York and sleeping on my father's couch a little more bearable, it was this pizza.

"I have to watch my brother tonight. It's my father and stepmother's anniversary." At least this time I wasn't lying. I'd promised them I'd babysit a week ago. You didn't break a promise to my stepmother and not expect some consequences. There were drill sergeants that ran sloppier barracks than Zola.

"If they get home early, you should swing by." He was still smiling. Two things about Pete—he wasn't a quitter, and he wasn't easily offended.

I was digging out money when he waved his hand.

"Don't worry about it. The boss took the afternoon off," he said, referring to his father. The man was a foot shorter than Pete, but size didn't matter. No one in the neighborhood messed with Old Sal.

"Thanks." I didn't put up much of a fight, since my bank

account was running on fumes. I didn't get paid for another couple of days, and Zola ruled the finances with an iron fist. She wasn't one to spot you a twenty without wanting a full accounting of where every dime of your money went first. I'd rather exist on whatever scraps I could find around the house than hand over my bank account or provide an inventory of my hair gel receipts. Yes, maybe I did overpay for hair products, but she should try to keep this mass of hair from frizzing. If she had this mess, what would *she* be willing to pay?

It didn't even matter that I'd pay it back. She felt that allowing me to sleep on the couch was concession enough to my survival.

Looking at the clock, I calculated she'd be home by now, so I'd be eating my slice here. If I didn't, I would have to face an onslaught of questions on how I had the money to eat out but hadn't saved up for an apartment yet. It was hard to save when I was still paying off the bill to bury my mother.

The door opened behind me, and Pete dropped the pizza cutter as he looked over my shoulder.

I glanced behind me, wondering who had managed to put Pete on edge. He had black hair and skin so tan I could practically smell the salty air of the Mediterranean ocean coming off him. He had the smooth movements of an athlete.

He nodded in my direction, those cool gray eyes setting me on edge once again. I'd never met this man until today, and now I'd seen him twice in one day. His card with his name and address, but nothing else, was still in the back pocket of my jeans.

He stopped at the counter and was glancing down at his phone as he said, "Have ten of our regular pies and three antipastos delivered in an hour."

He barely acknowledged me with a minuscule nod in my

direction. Maybe that was why I couldn't seem to ignore his presence. Men who had never met me before typically gave me a little more attention than this one did. Even our first meeting was more of a courtesy on his part than anything else.

I continued eating my slice, not caring that he'd written me off as being beneath his notice. I had enough problems in my life, and his attention would definitely add to them. Some guys were like that. The smell of trouble oozed from their pores.

I'd grabbed a stool at the counter when he tilted his head in my direction. "Put whatever she wants on my tab as well."

So he was willing to admit I was living, breathing, and standing beside him. He just didn't care to offer up a polite *hello* or *good to see you again.* Either way, I didn't need his free food like he was throwing a coin to a lowly peon in the street.

"That's not necessary—"

"It is." The man nailed me with a stare that stole my voice.

Fine. He felt better buying me some pizza I was already getting for free? So be it. He could think he was the big man.

He turned to leave, but not before he stopped in front of me. "Remember, you have my card."

"Yes. Thank you," I said, knowing I'd never use it.

He walked out, and I couldn't seem to stop myself from staring at his back. There was an interesting backstory there for sure. He was one of those people that was almost born to attract, or maybe repel, like he had a gravity all his own.

"You know him?" Pete asked as soon as the door shut.

"Not really. Some kid at the rink was being hassled by some older kids. I intervened. It wasn't a big deal, but that man came in later and thanked me. I think he was the kid's uncle or something."

That wasn't exactly how it went down, but it was the heart of the situation. It was easier than explaining the oddity of the meeting. How he'd walked in, handed me a card with a name and an address, and said, "If you ever need anything, and I mean *anything*, come see me."

That last "anything" had seemed a bit overdone. I'd gotten the impression his idea of "anything" didn't necessarily preclude illegal activities or violence. By the time he'd walked out of the rink, I had a chill so bad I was like one of those old, frosted ice cream containers.

"Why? You know him?" I asked, curious in spite of my better judgment.

Pete shook his head a little too fast and vigorously. "We don't talk about him, or any of them."

Them? Don't ask. Don't. Ask.

"What do you mean—"

"I can't have this discussion. I'm serious. But if I were you, I'd steer clear." Pete took a few steps away, checking a pizza he'd just put in the oven.

I was better off not knowing anyway. I went back to eating my pizza, which needed just a tad more crushed pepper seeds.

The sound of a body crashing into the worktable across from me jerked my attention from the slice I was doctoring. Leaning over the counter, I spotted Pete lying on the tiled floor.

I didn't think, just rushed around the counter calling his name. I dropped to my knees beside him, grabbed his skinny shoulders, and began shaking him, but he was lifeless. No heartbeat, no pulse, no breath. No screams or moans. No warning of any kind. One second Pete was alive and standing there, and then he was dead on the ground.

"Help! Somebody call 911!" I yelled as I began to pound on his chest, doing what I could remember from a CPR class I'd taken three years ago.

A high-pitched scream came from the other side of the counter that separated the work space from the dining room. I stood, seeing most of the other patrons were also littering the ground, lifeless. Only seconds ago they had been enjoying a meal at the end of a workday. The only exception was a lone guy who was looking at his friends and screaming over and over.

I'd barely taken in the horror of Pete and the screaming guy when I heard the sounds of crashing outside. The loud car alarms added to the feeling of dread in the air.

I ran outside and almost tripped over the body of a pretty blond woman still holding the tiny hand of her child. Both lay lifeless in front of the pizzeria door. Cars were careening around the streets like they were part of some impromptu demolition derby. The ones not veering off to crash into store-fronts were a tangled pile of hoods smashed into trunks or vehicles t-boned into one another. The people piloting the cars may have stopped functioning, but the cars were still wrecking balls, forming blockades on either side of the road.

A man walked out of the post office across the street, looking as dazed as I was.

"What the hell is going on?" He had his fist twisted in his hair, and looked across the street at me as if I had an answer.

"I don't know." I stood there, just shaking my head and whispering to myself, "I don't know, I don't know."

As I stared at the chaos surrounding me, an urgency to get somewhere safe and familiar pushed me to move.

I had to get home.

My car was parked in front of the pizzeria, but the street

was clogged with cars piled into each other. The sidewalks weren't much better.

What started as a jog turned into a run toward home. The cacophony of car alarms, and the roar of engines racing from the constant pressure of a dead foot on the pedal, was deafening. At the corner, I spied a bike on its side—the rider lay lifeless on the pitted and stained concrete. The bike wasn't doing her any good. I felt a jolt of shock at how quickly such a cold and callous thought popped into my head. That didn't stop me from pulling the bike out from the under her and throwing my purse in the pink basket before riding off.

It was ten miles to my building, and the entire way, the same terrifying scenes of destruction and death played over and over again. People lying on the ground, lifeless, and cars either crashed into one another or drifted off the street to plant themselves into buildings. I hopped off the bike at my building and then took the stairs two at a time to the fourth floor. I was afraid if I took the elevator and got stuck, no one would come for me.

I swung the door open to the sight of my stepmother collapsed on the living room floor. Charlie, my younger brother, was hugging her lifeless body, crying. My father was sitting on the floor, his back against the sofa and his phone at his side. The sound of ringing coming from his cell was the only other noise in the room.

"She just dropped," he said. "I called for an ambulance, but no one will answer."

My legs refused to support me, and I fell to my knees beside her, staring at her body, unable to do anything but stare at her. How many people were dead? Was it just this area? Just New York? The U.S.? What had happened?

I was still frozen in panic when I felt Charlie's little arms wrap around me, clinging to *me* for support. That was when it really hit that this was about as bad as it got. If I was someone's safe harbor in a storm, we were all going to die.

Chapter Two

THE DAY AFTER...

Yesterday, ninety percent of the world had died. Ninety. Percent. That's what was being said. The official news on the television was gone, but there were a few people getting the word out on the radio. Some had managed to connect to people on other continents. Word was the bulk of the world had died in one fell swoop. There was nowhere to go to escape this, and no one knew why it had happened.

To say it was bringing out the worst in some people would be the understatement of the century. I could hear the fighting start last night in the streets. Gunshots and screams replaced the more normal sounds of traffic and car radios.

Looking out the window, I could see a dead man with a knife sticking out of his chest on the corner of our street. That sight yesterday morning would have had me reaching for the phone. Today, there was no one to call.

My father, Michael McDermott, was pacing in the living

room as Charlie sat beside me on the couch. He had my arm locked against his small body just in case I got the notion to leave him alone with this crazy person that looked like his dad but acted like a stranger.

"What's going to happen?" Dad asked yet again. He'd been mumbling the same question or similar versions of it for the last few hours as he paced.

He didn't stop moving, pacing back and forth to the point he was making me dizzy.

"It'll be fine." That was a whopper of a lie, but someone had to pretend the world was okay for the kid. Did my father have to have a meltdown like this in front of him? Did he not see his son sitting here? Staring at him with terror? His little eyes had enlarged to several times their normal size as he stared at me, ready to cling to any shred of hope.

"The world is over. *Nothing* is going to be fine." Dad threw his arms out in a clear sign of defeat.

"You don't know that. We will get through this." Wow, I was becoming a whopper of a liar, but it had to be done.

Charlie was looking up at me, trying to measure who he believed, the liar or the lunatic. He snuggled closer, seeming to have chosen sides. It wasn't much of a win, considering my competition.

My father ran both his hands through his hair, making the thick honey-blond locks stick straight upward. If I didn't have his hair, I wasn't sure there'd be any resemblance at all, physically or emotionally.

He'd always cracked under pressure. As a child, I had instinctively known my mother was the one to go to with any problems. He'd looked to her the same way I had, the person to go to when he screwed up and needed saving. It wasn't a surprise that he'd had a past riddled with drugs. That was how

I'd ended up with my mother on the other side of the country, just so she could excise him from our lives as much as possible.

I'd resented it once upon a time, but the picture was getting very clear, very fast.

But that was years ago. He was older now. He'd work his way out of this panic and be stronger, step up and do what was needed, if not for me then for Charlie. If he didn't, I'd have to. One of us had to do *something*. I might not have been a survivalist, but instinct told me inaction would lead to death as surely as whatever had killed the majority of the world.

"We need to go scavenge for some things before it gets harder to find stuff," I said, trying to keep my voice calm for Charlie.

My father kept pacing, not acknowledging that I'd spoken, or maybe he was so wound up in his own panic that he didn't hear me. Our civilization had ground to a halt, and all he was doing was wearing a path in the carpet. If I hadn't forced him to carry out his wife's dead body, he might've been tripping over her corpse right now.

One of us had to step up, and if it wasn't going to be the fifty-year-old, it would be the twenty-year-old. I was going to have to get out there and get supplies, find us something to live off before it was all taken. More importantly, go find Charlie insulin. Because if I didn't, no one else was going to.

It was an unpleasant reality, because I didn't want to take care of anyone. I wanted the luxury of falling apart, or at least only worrying about myself.

I watched him do yet another lap and realized how close he was to breaking. I wasn't sure I should even leave Charlie with him, but there weren't any alternatives at the moment.

"You stay here with Charlie. I'm going to see if I can find

us some food. And you know Charlie needs his insulin. We need to stockpile as much as we can find." I side-eyed my little brother. Charlie was too young to understand the medicine keeping him alive was no longer going to be produced and what that meant for him.

"No, no," Dad said, something finally triggering his full attention. Maybe he was going to wake up to protect his son. "You stay here. I should be the one to go out."

I wasn't convinced, but Charlie's fingers were digging into my arm so hard I wasn't sure I'd be able to detangle him and leave anyway.

"Okay, but you should go now." I glanced down at Charlie and added, "People are already on the hunt for the same things we are, so you need to get moving."

My father nodded, seeming to calm down as he was prodded into action. He was grabbing bags and heading toward the door. Maybe he would surprise me after all?

"Don't be too long, okay?"

He nodded but didn't look or say anything else as he walked out. The lack of commitment left a knot in my stomach the size of the Rock of Gibraltar.

It was eight o'clock. My father had left eleven hours ago. I couldn't sit here any longer hoping he was doing the right thing. That wasn't who he was. It had never been him.

Why wasn't I moving? Because I was stalling. It was easier to sit here and be mad at him than go out there. I was as bad as him, grasping for excuses not to go out and do what I had to.

I could feel Charlie watching me, constantly trying to gauge how terrifying this new world was by whether I was freaking out. I glanced over at him and smiled. He went back to his game. Inside, where he couldn't see, I was having a full-blown panic attack.

I was twenty. I was too young for the world to end. I couldn't take care of myself. How was I supposed to take care of him?

But if I didn't, he was dead. My father wasn't going to step up. There was a reason he gravitated toward strong, borderline controlling women. He wasn't capable of taking care of himself, let alone his son. Left to his own devices, he would always default to giving up without a fight.

If I didn't get myself in gear, I was dead, and Charlie along with me. We. Were. All. Dead.

The main door below the window I was staring out opened again as some of the younger male survivors from the building carried out another body and tossed it onto a wheelbarrow. I'd lost count around twenty.

They were wheeling them away, heading down the street in the direction of a cemetery. There might've been a rotting pile, or maybe they'd dug a mass grave. I didn't particularly care to know either way. I was already on information overload.

We'd all figured out pretty fast that no one was coming to get them. Everyone had lost someone, usually more than one. Some families had been wiped out entirely. If they didn't clear the building, the stench would drive out the living soon.

"What are you looking at?" Charlie walked over, trying to climb up onto the bench with me. I scooped him up and headed for the couch. Last thing I wanted was for him to watch dead bodies being wheeled down the street.

"Nothing. Hey, want to watch one of your movies?" I suggested the entertainment like it was going to be the best hour and a half he'd ever spend.

I had a few of his favorites downloaded on my tablet for him, and luckily we still had electricity. I grabbed my tablet from the table, where I'd left it plugged in, scared the electricity would turn off at any moment.

"When's Daddy coming back?" he said as I got him settled on the couch and handed him the movie.

Tough question to answer, but it was better than earlier this morning, when he asked why everyone died, or last night, when he was asking why his mommy was dead.

"Hopefully he's getting things for us and will be back soon." I ran my index finger softly down his cheek.

If he didn't, I would be going soon, and I'd have to find someone to leave him with and go alone. Our peaceful, low-crime neighborhood had turned into bedlam in less than twenty-four hours, and it would be hard enough to stay safe on my own without a five-year-old tagging along.

"Can I play with Eddie tomorrow?"

Eddie, his playmate one floor below, who he went to kindergarten with. Or had.

"I think they left." *Left* wasn't the most accurate description, but it was better than telling him the entire family had been carried out on a wheelbarrow moments ago.

"Is he coming back?"

"I don't think so."

Something had caused this world to purge most of its population, and there didn't seem to be any rhyme or reason to it. How did you have a conversation like that with a five-year-old?

There was a knock at the door, and I jumped. Every noise was doing that to me lately.

I went to the door, looked through the peephole, and saw Frank, one of the other tenants in the building. He didn't seem much older than my twenty years. We'd had a few passing hellos in the months I'd been here, but that had been about it until the last couple of days.

He was the only one in his family who'd survived Death Day, but that wasn't an unusual situation. Having anyone left was an anomaly.

"Hey, I just wanted to let you know me and some of the guys are organizing," he said when I opened the door. He glanced down at Charlie, smiling before he said, "We're checking some of the empty places out, you know, making sure there's nothing left to create a problem. Help some of the residents empty out trash cans before the garbage might start to cause an issue. Do you need any assistance?" He was looking over my shoulder, like he was casing the place.

"No. We're fine. I still have my father. He did what had to be done last night."

"Oh yeah. I saw him. Your stepmother, right?" he asked, soft enough that Charlie wouldn't hear.

"Yes."

My father had wanted to wait, kept thinking he'd be able to get an ambulance on the phone, or someone to come and get her. He hadn't seen the bodies drop all at once. He'd been clinging to hope, but I'd sent him on his way with a dead body and shovel to the nearest cemetery. I had a feeling whoever's plot we'd taken wasn't going to be around to put up a fight.

"You?" I asked.

"I'm the only one left." For a moment, a lost look came into Frank's eyes.

"I'm sorry." I was. No matter my personal feelings about Frank, it sucked losing your whole family.

He nodded and then shrugged it off. He was probably

compartmentalizing. If you wanted to survive what was happening, it was going to be a much-needed skill.

"I'm not sure if you noticed, but me and some of the other guys set up a watch at all the entrances." He leaned a forearm on the frame of the door, leaning in ever so slightly.

"I did. Thank you." I nodded, forcing myself not to take a step back. I wasn't sure why, but this conversation felt a little like dealing with a feral dog, and I didn't want to show fear.

"We do what we can. Got to stick together, right?" He was smiling, and although it was fast, his eyes slipped to my breasts.

"Yes. Of course."

"Let me know if you need anything else, okay?" He smiled so wide I saw more gum than teeth.

"Thanks."

I shut and locked the door as soon as he left.

The night came and went with no sign of my father.

Chapter Three

IT WAS five o'clock the next night and my father still hadn't come back. Maybe he was dead. That thought should've upset me more than it did. Maybe I was compartmentalizing as well. Too bad I couldn't block off my panic, but that seemed to be a little bit more stubborn.

I could sit here and panic, waiting for my father to return, or I could do something. Anything was better than sitting here waiting. A strength that I'd thought died with my mother seemed to be waking up, stirring me to get moving.

"Charlie, go grab a few toys. We need to go check on Widow Herbert." I felt a twinge of guilt that I hadn't already checked on the elderly lady out of friendship. The guilt might have stung a little more because the only reason I was going now was to ask for a favor.

He tilted his head as if what I was saying sounded bizarre, but then got up anyway.

I went into the kitchen and grabbed my pepper spray out of my purse and the scariest-looking knife I could find. I hid them from my brother in a cloth shopping bag.

Charlie came back from his room with his backpack filled with enough toys to last a month.

"Can I bring Graham?" he asked, holding up his teddy bear in his other hand.

"Definitely."

He hadn't let it go since this had begun. I wished I had a Graham. I'd be lugging around a whole bag of stuffed animals if they made me feel better.

I tugged Charlie past the elevators.

"We're taking the stairs?" he asked.

"Yes. From here on out, elevators aren't reliable, so never get on one. If Daddy tells you to, tell him I said you can't."

"But what happens when you leave?" There was a hitch in his voice and a look of panic in his eyes.

Before Death Day, I was going to move out as soon as I could. This had never been a long-term plan. But that was then, and nothing was the same now. Charlie didn't understand that this was it. For everyone. In the blink of an eye, everyone's future had been torched.

"I'm not leaving you." If I did, he'd never make his sixth birthday. I hadn't been able to save my mother, but damned if I wouldn't do better by him.

"Promise?"

I looked down at his big hazel eyes and then ruffled his honey-colored hair, both the same shades as mine. It also threw me a little, how we looked more alike than either of us did to our father.

"I swear. Where I go, you go. It's us from here on out, okay?"

He nodded fast and then grabbed my hand. He gripped me as tight as he could, as if I might change my mind if he didn't agree vigorously enough.

I walked to Widow Herbert's place and knocked. I'd run into her more than a few times over the past few months I'd lived here. Even though she was in her nineties, we'd instantly connected on some strange level. Hopefully that connection was strong enough to ask a favor now. If she was still alive.

"Piper!" she said, smiling and swinging the door open. "So nice to have a visitor. And look, you brought Charlie."

The wave of relief at seeing the elderly woman was more intense than I'd expected. It was as if a tiny bit of the weight I'd been carrying lifted.

There were noises down the hall, doors opening and shutting. Widow Herbert glanced in the direction they were coming from and then motioned us in with a hurried wave. She shut the door quickly, locking it as if she suspected more unwelcome bodies would be passing this way as well.

"Would you like to have a cup of tea with me? I just brewed some." She was dressed in her normal matching jogging outfit, her gray hair swept up into a bun, as if today were just any old day of the week.

"Actually, I need to go out and check on a few things, and my father isn't around. Could I possibly leave Charlie here for a little while? I'll share anything I might find," I said.

I barely knew this woman and had shown up with a big ask. She might've looked great for her nineties, and seemed self-sufficient, but I was dumping a kid on her.

"Charlie, will you help me check on all my clocks? I'm not sure they're working right. I've got some snacks after you're finished as a reward." She motioned to her living room, which had walls lined with cuckoo clocks. I couldn't imagine the kind of noise that many cuckoo clocks would create on the hour, every hour.

Charlie ran into the living room like he'd just been let loose in a toy store.

"My late husband Walter loved cuckoo clocks," she said wistfully.

"You don't mind?" I asked.

"Not at all. I love the company, especially now without even the television to keep me entertained. Come sit with me before you leave? I was just pouring myself some tea."

I looked at the door but then nodded. I'd just dumped a five-year-old on her. If she wanted to talk to me, I'd talk. Actually, I *wanted* to talk. I felt like I was bursting with words. I only had a five-year-old to talk to, and he'd be traumatized by the truth.

"Frank and some of the other guys who are left are cleaning out the apartments," I said, sitting down in her kitchen. I wasn't sure why I was bringing this up, but it wasn't just small talk. Something about it bothered me, but I couldn't quite say why he set my teeth on edge.

"You mean ransacking the empty ones for food and anything his little gang can trade for their own personal use? Knowing him, that sounds about right." She was still smiling as she poured me tea.

"They've set up guards at the entrances, too." I wasn't sure why I tried to defend him. It sure as heck wasn't because I liked or trusted him.

"I was a clinical psychologist for forty years. There are many things I don't know, but people aren't one of them. Frank will take advantage of this situation, including us if he can." She pushed a container of almond milk toward me.

"I'm fine." It was a tiny container, and I waved her off, not wanting to take the last of her supplies.

"See these little things? Shelf stable. They last for years. I have a stockpile of them. Use some."

Was Widow Herbert some secret prepper type?

"How's your father holding up?" The question was innocent enough, but for all Widow Herbert's years, she was as sharp as a brand-new razor.

I shrugged. It was all she needed, and I didn't have the heart to put his failings on blast while I was still coming to terms with them myself.

"And Charlie? I know he has certain needs," she said, nodding toward the living room.

"Looks like the buck stops here." My fingers shook, and I put the cup down, rattling it against its saucer as I did. "What's going to happen? What is going to become of this world?"

She took a deep breath, as if preparing to tell me things she didn't particularly care to say. She also wasn't the type to dodge the truth.

"When you lose ninety percent of your population in one fell swoop, there aren't enough people left alive to sustain the grid, the water system, the sewer systems. We'll be living in the dark ages soon. It's impossible to say when the first glitch will happen and no one will be there to fix it, but we're on borrowed time.

"Some things will stop faster than others, depending on the situation and how many people are left trying to keep things going. Point is, though, we need electricity to run almost everything. Even the water to this building gets pumped with electricity."

I picked up my cup with two hands to try to control the shaking. Widow Herbert seemed to be waiting for me to get under control. She'd be waiting a while.

"And then what?" I asked.

"Hard to say exactly how it'll play out, but it'll probably go something like it has throughout history." She lifted her hand in the air in a flippant kind of way, as if she weren't living through this as well. "For example, when Rome fell, the feudal system rose. It started with small communities banding together and then grew from there.

"Something similar will happen now as well. Survivors will begin to group together, for better or worse. People will step into the power vacuum. The world will go on, just differently. The only constant in life is that things change." She smiled again. How come she was so calm? How could she speak of this like it wasn't the end of the line? Our world was crashing down around us, and she was brewing tea like it was any other afternoon.

"How can you be so calm?"

She leaned forward and covered my hand. "I'm ninety-six years old. Life doesn't owe me a thing."

Chapter Four

I HOPPED onto my pink bike and did a quick prayer of thanks to the girl who'd owned it. The closest pharmacy was only a five-minute bike ride away. The lights were all on but the doors had busted glass. I hid my bike between two trucks and approached with my pepper spray in one hand and a knife in the other.

The lights in the store were on and the door was wide open. I approached cautiously. A young girl, probably no older than sixteen, was digging through a pile of tampon boxes on the floor.

She looked up as I walked in, sizing me up. I lifted my hands, trying to signal to her that I wasn't looking for a problem. She gave me a nod. I pointed in the direction of the noise on the other side of the store.

"Some old guy looking for heartburn meds," she said. "Most everything worth anything is gone."

"Thanks." I headed toward the pharmacy anyway, refusing to leave until I checked it out myself. Food wouldn't matter to

Charlie if I couldn't find him a large stash of insulin. Type one diabetics couldn't live without it.

If the majority of the store was picked over, the pharmacy was wiped clean. Other than a few blood pressure cuffs and a lone pregnancy test, there was nothing left. I'd been afraid to leave Charlie alone. I'd held on to hope that my father would do the right thing, and now there wasn't any insulin. I wasn't delusional enough to think this was going to be a one-off situation.

A wrapper crinkled, and I jerked around, finding the girl who had been by the tampons standing there.

"Do you know what's going to happen?" she asked. "I live around the corner, and my family is dead. My neighbors won't answer their door. I don't know what to do."

She looked terrified. She looked the way I felt. If I had a safe place for her, I might've taken her home with me. I didn't. My building might be a worse situation than her being on her own.

"What's your name?"

"Eveline," she said, taking another step toward me.

"You live close to here?"

"Down on Mulnochy. Number six."

I committed her address to memory, swearing to myself that I'd jot it down as soon as I got home in case I forgot.

"If you know which neighbors are dead, get their stuff and then find a good place to hide it. Gather every speck of food you can find, stuff that will last, like cans and dried foods. Take whatever guns and ammo you find as well. Eventually things will fall into some sort of organized situation, but I don't know if it'll be good or bad. You just need to lie low for now. If I find somewhere safe, I'll come and get you, okay?"

She nodded but continued to stare at me. "Can't I come with you now?"

"I don't have a good place to bring you." The way Frank had been looking at me, I couldn't willingly bring back a kid into that situation. I was old enough to know what might come next. Bringing her there was like leading a lamb to slaughter.

"But I'm scared to be alone." She started to sniffle.

"I can't." I could barely take care of myself, and now Charlie. I moved toward the door, and tears started streaming down her face. "I'll come and get you once I figure some things out. Just…lie low."

She kept crying. I couldn't bring her with me. Not there. The writing was on the wall. We'd all have to get out of there soon.

"I'm sorry. I promise I'll come and get you if I find a place to go."

She wouldn't stop staring at me as tears spilled down her cheeks.

I had to leave. I didn't have a choice. I got back on my bike, saying another small prayer to the unknown girl who'd owned the bike and now another for Eveline, and then headed to the next pharmacy.

Eight pharmacies later and more empty shelves. This pharmacy was nestled in one of those big-box stores. I'd come on a lark, knowing it would be hit early. Talk about a time for wanting things supersized. I didn't think there were enough people left to wipe out supplies in every place, but I guess desperation turned everyone into hoarders.

I scanned the rest of the store and then, on a whim, checked near the cash registers. There was a box of cereal and a loaf of potato bread on the floor of the last checkout station.

The cereal box was open and the bread was partially squashed, and I was happy to have both.

I grabbed the items just as the lights in the place died. I looked toward the front windows. The street lights had gone out too.

I walked out onto the street and looked around. It had never been so dark in my life. I might never see a lit street again. There might never be electricity again in my lifetime. This wasn't just the aftermath of a storm, or a war. This was the new reality for the foreseeable future. From this point on, we were all living in the shadow of death, and it knocked the wind out of me like a punch to the gut.

I climbed back on my bike with the cereal and bread buried in the basket underneath my bag, said my prayer to the unknown girl, and biked home in utter darkness.

Chapter Five

I MADE another X on the calendar. It had been nine days since Death Day, the official marking of the end of the world. My stepmother had been one of those throwbacks who'd liked having a physical calendar. I ran a hand over it now. There was something comforting about being able to track the dates. Like a useless anchor, too short to hit the bottom of the chasm we were all adrift in, and yet somehow it provided a mild sense of ease anyway.

I looked at the days ahead marked with a check. Four checks. That was it. Four days' worth of insulin left, and there wasn't a pharmacy anywhere within fifty miles that hadn't been wiped clean. I knew because I'd checked every one of them. Why hadn't they been better stocked?

The door opened and my father walked in, his features slack and his skin ashen. He'd shown up the day after I took Charlie to Widow Herbert. No explanation as to where he'd been and nothing to show for the time he'd been away. He looked exhausted, but it wasn't from going out and searching for insulin or food. No, he hadn't brought a thing home since Death Day.

"Where were you? What? You spent all this time out and couldn't find anything? *Again?*" I gave him a slow once-over.

He walked over to the couch and sat, his eyelids drooping as if he were going to fall asleep right then and there.

"I went looking but there was nothing." He nodded, as if my words had finally sunk in, but his brain seemed to have glazed over the anger simmering in my words.

It was easier when he didn't come back for days. He'd only steal whatever I'd brought home for his drugs. A small packet fell out of his pocket and onto the couch cushion. He wasn't tired. He was high. The world was falling apart, and instead of stepping up, he was falling down with it.

"Charlie, come on, it's time to go." It was bad enough that Charlie had to watch his mother die. Now his father was self-destructing when his child needed him most.

"Can I have a snack before bed?" Charlie grabbed Graham off the floor where he'd been playing and walked over to me.

My chest tightened and my stomach growled, as if seconding his complaint. The only reason he'd eaten at all today was because Widow Herbert had given me some of her stash to feed Charlie. She tried to offer me some as well, but I'd lied and insisted I wasn't hungry. I drew the line at taking a free meal from a woman in her nineties.

I ruffled his shaggy brown hair. "We don't have anything tonight, but I'll get you something extra-special tomorrow." I didn't know what that was going to be, but I'd find *something*. "Did you brush your teeth?"

"Why do I have to brush my teeth? We used up the last of the toothpaste this morning."

"We're going to use water in the meantime, and I'll get

toothpaste tomorrow." Certain items like that were easier to find if you weren't too picky about the condition.

I nudged him toward the bathroom. He held his toothbrush over the sink, and I used the gallon of water I'd collected to wet it. After catching the overflow in a pan, I carefully poured it into a glass to save for later.

We lost the water when we lost electricity. I'd been collecting water from the numerous freshwater lakes Staten Island had. Boiling it took time, but it gave me the feeling of doing something positive. The sewers were still functioning, but I wasn't sure how long that would last. Once they went, we'd really have to get out of the city. I'd leave now if I could figure out a way off this island with a kid and a woman in her nineties.

"It's late. Where are you going?" my father asked, his head lolling around on his shoulders, as we came back into the living room.

"I have to go out. We have no food. The cans of soup I brought back are already gone. So is the bag of rice, the beans, and the toothpaste. Not to mention we're also almost out of insulin. Things are disappearing faster than I can get them." I pointedly looked at his arms, and the marks on them.

He started crying. "I'm sorry. I didn't mean to take those things. I'm going to be better. I swear. It's just I can't stop seeing her standing there one second and then—"

"I know. We have to go."

Charlie glued himself to my leg. My father wasn't the only one who'd lost her. Instead of trying to pull it together for Charlie, he just became *this*. He didn't even try to help himself, let alone his children. No, it was all about *him*, and *his* pain. What *he* needed.

"Piper, I'm not strong like you," he said.

Did he think I wanted to be strong? Didn't he think I'd like to sit on the couch and have the luxury of crying and falling apart? But I couldn't because, unlike him, I cared about what happened to Charlie. He'd made a different choice.

I picked Charlie up, feeling his little body trembling. "I have to leave."

I made it to the stairwell before I put him down. "What's wrong with Daddy? Why do I always sleep at Widow Herbert's now?" he asked, clinging to my hand.

Because your father is too doped up to function. Because he is a loser who'd rather get high than step up for his family. Because your father is a scumbag.

Of course, I couldn't say any of those things. I'd have to frost over this mud pie and doll it up enough for a five-year-old to be able to handle it.

"Remember how I told you that a lot of people got sick and it changed the world? Well, not all of them died. Some of them just changed, like Daddy."

"Is that why he's tired all the time? 'Cause he's changed?"

"Yes. It makes him very tired."

He might not have believed me, but he stopped asking questions.

Widow Herbert was already poking her head out, waiting for us as we walked down the hallway toward her place.

She let us in silently, with just a pat on my shoulder as I passed. I got Charlie settled on her couch, tucking the blankets up to his chin and then karate-chopping them all around.

"Okay, you're protected now," I said.

"Promise you'll never leave me?" he asked.

That wasn't a promise I should make. One lesson we'd all learned from Death Day was that we didn't know what was coming. Every night, it was a coin toss whether I'd make it back alive.

But try telling that to a terrified five-year-old and see how well he handled it.

"I'll never leave you." *Please, God, don't let me be a liar. Not about this, at least. Let this one thing be true.*

I waited until his breathing calmed, knowing that keeping that promise might be impossible.

Widow Herbert walked in with her knitting and sat on the end of the couch.

"I'll be back as soon as I can," I said to her.

Her brows rose. "Don't worry about time. Just be careful."

I nodded.

I was leaving the building when Frank caught sight of me. Roger and Timmy, two of his newfound "friends," were walking into a nearby apartment that I knew they didn't live in.

Frank left them and headed toward me.

"Piper, got a second?" he asked, and we both knew I couldn't say no.

"Sure. What's going on?" I tried to avoid looking at his friends and focused on hiding my distaste.

"The guys and I have been talking. Between carrying out the bodies and setting up a watch, we're running out of time to do much else. We'd really appreciate it if everyone in the building could kick in to offset what we need, since we don't have the time or energy to go out and scavenge ourselves. Just like a percentage of what you're bringing in for overhead. You know, like a tax of sorts for services rendered."

Even as we stood there, I could see his other two guys carrying out bags of anything worthwhile in the unit. Everyone in the building knew that they were taking anything of value from the units they could, and no one had said a word because they had been carrying out the bodies and guarding the place.

They were now set up better than anyone else in the surrounding area, and they wanted more.

I stood there, my mind blanking on what to do. If I said something, called them out on what they were doing, there was nothing stopping them from kicking us out of the apartment. Or worse. They could kill Charlie, or kill me, which would be a death sentence for him anyway. There was no police, no government—we were truly on our own.

"Yeah, sure. I understand." I understood all too well. We were going to have to get out of here, because with no one to hold them in check, the demands would be increasing. But where to go? It wasn't just me anymore. Almost overnight, I had a five-year-old to care for as well. It was clear my father wouldn't be doing it.

"We'll need it within a day. Guys are getting hungry, you know?"

I nodded. "Got it."

I walked out of the building before he could lay on anymore demands. I ducked into the first shadowed nook I could find, my breathing ragged.

I could handle this. I'd get us out of this mess because there was no other option. I wouldn't go down like my father, sitting on the couch getting high.

I pulled the card out of my back pocket, the one I'd gotten on Death Day. The one I'd taken to carrying around with me. If the man who had given me this was still alive, he'd be flourishing. There were some people who thrived in chaos, and he'd be one of them. I just had to pray he was among the living and still willing to honor his word.

Pete had acted like that mysterious man was a person to be

avoided at all costs, and that had been *before* Death Day, when the world was still considered at least somewhat safe and civilized. Now what would he be like? Although I guess when you're already living with such low standards to begin with, it's just another day at the shop.

If I had to drop my standards to survive, more importantly, to take care of Charlie, I would. I'd get in with the worst pack of murderers and thieves around. The stores and pharmacies had all been cleared out, and there was no doubt that this man would be sitting on some of the stash. I didn't know where our next meal would come from, and Charlie was almost out of insulin. There were no alternatives left.

I dug my bike out of the sticker bushes and hopped on, sending my silent prayer to the unknown girl, hoping she was watching down on me and that I'd survive the night.

Chapter Six

I LISTENED for sounds as I watched the bridge up ahead. Word was that a gang was robbing anyone who passed here. Just last week, someone died trying to cross. None of that mattered because to get to the address on the card, I had to get to the other side. I was *going* to cross this bridge, whether it was a good idea or not.

I watched, my heart beating even as I stood still. I'd been waiting for a half an hour already, debating when to try.

A motorcycle sounded in the distance, and I tucked myself further behind the building. Not many people used cars anymore because ninety percent of the streets were impassable. Motorcycles, on the other hand, were a hot commodity. I watched as it approached. If it made it across, crossing right after was my best chance.

The motorcycle came zooming closer, and just as my hopes grew, a chain running across the entire width of the bridge was jerked upward a few feet off the ground. The motorcyclist tried to turn to avoid it, but it was too close. The motorcycle fell on its side and slid with the rider.

The rider wasn't going down so easy, though. He was on his feet in seconds, as a swarm of four men ran forward, surrounding him. The rider had a gun in each hand, and the ambushers eyed him up.

This was it. Try to pass as they were all distracted or not go at all. Since not going wasn't an option, I pedaled like I was being chased by the demons of hell. I didn't look as they screamed in my direction and then a man jumped in front of me. A shot went off, and his body fell as I swerved to miss him.

I slowed, looking at the motorcycle guy, knowing I owed him. If I'd seen someone in trouble before Death Day, there wouldn't have been a question about helping them. Now, every single action was weighed.

"Go," he yelled.

I still hesitated, but then he smiled as another ambusher neared him. The guy was off his rocker.

The other three ambushers were frozen, unsure of what to do next.

"Thank you," I screamed before I pedaled like my life depended on it, which it probably did.

"Anytime, kid," the guy yelled back.

I slowed to catch my breath but didn't stop pedaling until I made it to my destination. Even if I didn't have the address, I would've known something was different as soon as I neared the area.

The world all around was breaking down into mayhem, but you wouldn't know it from this street. Yes, there were no lights or electricity, but there was a calmness, a serenity here, that wasn't found anywhere else.

The old brick building on the corner matched the address: 214 News Blvd. I'd just been playing a game with Charlie, where you matched numbers to the letter in the alphabet. If you did it with 214, this place would be BAD News Blvd. What were the odds? Right now, probably high.

I peeked in the door window but couldn't make out much because of the way the glass was cut. I waited for my stomach to stop grumbling and then knocked. No one answered, so I knocked again. When that was ignored, I opened the door, hoping I wasn't going to get shot before they asked who I was.

The first thing that struck me was the amount of oil lamps burning, like they had fuel to spare. Even rich folk, or people who had been considered rich before the world fell apart, weren't this careless with their resources.

It looked like it was some kind of corner bar, except it didn't have any signage. A private club of some sorts?

There were two guys I didn't recognize sitting in the corner booth. One with the fairest hair I'd ever seen, sitting with a guy with dark skin and even darker eyes. They looked like they could've been an angel and a demon hanging out together, except I'd always been good at spotting danger. They both looked lethal.

"We're not open to the public," Angel said, giving me a once-over as if trying to decipher why someone like me would be somewhere like this. As if I should've known better.

"I'm looking for a job." I straightened, trying to look sturdier than I was, and definitely stronger than I felt.

"We don't need anyone," Demon said.

I didn't budge. Desperation had a way of making you braver than you really were, and if it were a sliding scale, I was about as brave as a person could get at the moment.

Another man walked out, this one with hair that could've been swapped out with a lion's mane.

"Who's this?" he asked the two guys in the booth.

"Some straggler that wants a job," Angel said. "We told her no, but she's still standing there for some reason."

Lion Mane walked toward me. He was every bit as big as the other two, but he didn't strike me as quite as dangerous, although he definitely wasn't safe. He seemed like he'd at least ask for your name before he stabbed you in the gut and let you bleed out like a pig.

His eyes ran the length of me. My boots were new. My clothes were clean, and I'd washed my hair in a nearby stream. The only thing that smelled of desperation was my thinness. I'd been average build a month ago, but lack of food had a way of dwindling a person down.

"*You* want to work here?" Lion Mane asked.

"Yes." I should've just pulled out the card and asked for Duncan, but some part of me wanted these guys who were obviously with him to see some sort of worth in me.

"Why?" Lion Mane asked, as if that was the most bizarre request he'd heard this year.

"Why does anyone work? I need things."

"Have you *heard* about us?" He was looking at me as if I might be off my rocker.

"I've heard rumors, but there's rumors about lots of people."

He accepted that with a shrug and then pointed to my eye. "What happened to your face?"

"I got punched." It had happened the day before yesterday and was looking uglier as it aged. I spent so little time worrying about my appearance these days that I'd almost forgotten about my fight with a guy over a bag of apples. I'd gotten to them first, but I left empty-handed and with a shiner for my efforts.

"By who?"

Why did he care? Did he think he'd know the guy? Did it have any bearing on this at all? These people were odd.

"I have no idea. Have you been outside recently? It's the fucking apocalypse. Who *hasn't* gotten punched might be the more pertinent question."

"You've got a point," he said, nodding. "Either way, it doesn't matter. We're not looking for help."

He turned to walk away, and I grabbed his arm. He stared at my hand as if shocked I'd touch him. I let go fast enough, but mostly to drag out the card. It would've been good to have gotten a job on my own. My current situation didn't leave room for standing on my pride, especially when that pride lent about as much support as a straw roof.

"I've got this." I pulled out the card from my back pocket and held it out to him. "This man said if I ever needed anything, I should come here and ask."

"Duncan gave this to you?" Lion Mane asked, holding the card and looking at me with a healthy dose of skepticism.

Did he think I'd plucked it out of the garbage or something?

"Yes." I grabbed the card out of his hand, like it had some sort of intrinsic value on its own. "Is he alive?"

"Yeah, he's still alive," Lion Mane said.

"What the hell could she have done that would've gotten one of Duncan's cards?" Angel said.

"She's cute, but Duncan isn't hard up. He doesn't need to pay favors for it," Demon said.

"Ew, no, we didn't, and he wasn't offering payment. I'm not a hooker," I replied, shooting him a look that should've set him back a few paces.

"Look at her, trying to show some claws!" Angel said, and they both laughed.

Lion Mane yelled toward a door at the back of the room, "Duncan!"

Duncan strolled out a few minutes later. I thought I saw a flicker of surprise in his eyes. Yeah, neither of us figured we'd ever see the other again, and that was before most people died. Before the end of the world, I would've kept a few miles in between us, but everything was different now.

"She's looking for a job. Says you know her," Lion Mane said.

"I do." Duncan walked forward, looking me over with that cool gaze that seemed to take in everything from the color of my boots to the flecks of green in my hazel eyes. "You want a job here?"

"I need stuff. You know, things I haven't been able to locate, but I think maybe you can." I sounded like an idiot, but something about this man staring at me was throwing me more off-kilter than a drunk standing on a kayak.

"And what is that?" A brow rose.

"Insulin."

He notched his head down a fraction of an inch and his nostrils flared. "But you're not a diabetic," he said, as if I'd told him I had a pair of horns on my head.

"It's for someone else." I crossed my arms. How he knew it wasn't for me didn't matter. All that counted was if he could get it.

"Why aren't they trying to get a job?" he asked.

"Because I am." I liked him better when he was ignoring me. It was a lot easier to think clearly.

He nodded, as if he somehow already guessed my issues, the weight I was carrying around.

"You crossed the bridge to get here?" he said.

"Yes." Again, how had he figured that out? Was he trying to gauge how desperate I was for the job? Very.

"When you cross again, tell them you're with me, or you won't be commuting here long."

"So I have a job?" I wanted to cry, collapse with relief, but I wasn't even moving because I couldn't believe it.

His shoulders rose and fell before he said, "Yes. I honor my debts." He looked at Lion Mane. "Buddie, give her what she needs. I've got other things to handle. I'll be back later." He nodded at me and walked out of the room.

My heart was racing, but this time from pure joy. I wanted to yell from the rooftops that I had a solution. I was going to get insulin.

Demon walked back over, the lines on his forehead deep and angry. "You need to understand, you don't repeat anything that goes on here, not who visits, what anyone says. Even if I get drunk and paranoid one night and think you have, you're dead, and I don't mean that as a figure of speech. And if you think Duncan will protect you, you're wrong."

He was nearly leaning over me, and the only reason I cared was that if I lost control and started jumping up and down in my joy, I might crack my head into his chin. He could blather on about how he was going to kill me. He could threaten me with torture first, too. I was hired. I was getting Charlie insulin.

"Can I have an advance on the insulin?" I asked Buddie, since he didn't scowl as much.

"Did you hear what I said? I'm not one to bluff. We've killed a lot of people, and we won't hesitate to kill some random girl who talks too much." Demon was pointing in my face.

"Rastin, lighten up," Buddie said.

Rastin didn't look like he was going to take that advice until he heard me agree.

"Yeah, I got it. I talk. You kill me. It's not a hard concept." I was waving both hands in the air. "Now, about the insulin? Do you have any or not?"

"You've got to give it to her, she's got balls," Buddie said, turning to Rastin.

Buddie had clearly never been as desperate as I had if he thought this was me being gutsy.

"We don't have it here, but I'll have it for you tomorrow when you come," Buddie said, trying to break the standoff between Rastin and me. Or technically, Rastin and who he thought I was. If he really knew me, he'd realize I didn't care a wink about his demands, his threats—really, anything other than insulin.

"I won't be in until night, though, okay? I've got other obligations during the day," I said, trying to address Buddie. Rastin already hated me anyway, so who cared what he thought?

Rastin was staring at me, debating whether to say something. Then he threw up his hands and looked at Buddie. "You deal with her," he said, and walked back toward Angel.

Buddie took a few steps toward the booth where his friends were sitting then glanced back over to see I hadn't moved.

"Was there something else?" he asked.

"Just curious, is this whole block your area? Or are some of these residences free game for scavenging?"

"Why? What do you want now?" Rastin asked.

I glanced at the booth, and the three of them were rolling their eyes and shaking their heads. Not only had desperation made me braver, it had obliterated my pride. I didn't care if their heads rolled off their shoulders.

"I need a bag of rice, or beans, or—something. I have to pay taxes."

"Didn't you just tell me it's 'the fucking apocalypse'? What taxes are you paying?" Buddie said.

"To the guy who's running the building where I live."

He stared at me for a second, his chest inflating and then sighing on a long whoosh of air. "Wait here."

He walked in the back and returned a minute later with a bag of oranges. No one had oranges at this point. It was like everyone had tried to gobble up all the fruit first, knowing it would go bad faster. We were all trying to savor what we might never have again.

"I don't have rice or beans handy, but this should do."

"Hey, what are you doing with my oranges? You know I like to snack on them," Angel said.

"Back off. She needs them," Buddie said.

Angel gave me a once-over, but something softened a hair. "Fine. Let her take them. But I'm eating your pistachios on principle."

"Thanks," I said to Buddie, shoving the oranges in my bag and hoping no one would see them on the ride back. "Thank you, Rastin and…"

Rastin and Angel just stared at me.

"We call the blond guy Birdie," Buddie said.

"Okay, well, thanks!" I waved in their direction.

Their expressions didn't change a bit. This was definitely going to be a hostile work environment, and I still couldn't quite keep the bounce out of my step as I left.

I rode my bike back, stopping right before the bridge.

"I'm with Duncan's crew. They said you can't screw with me," I yelled.

There was silence and then some rustling from the bushes.

"Why are we supposed to believe that?" a voice asked.

"You don't have to take my word for it. They're close by. Have one of your people go run and ask. I'll wait here while we see if they come back alive after you tell them you wouldn't let me pass."

Duncan's men had just met me, but I'd guarantee they wouldn't overlook an insult to their name. No. If Duncan gave his protection and someone ignored that? Well, I wasn't sure what they'd do, but I wouldn't want to be the person who found out.

The guy on the bridge didn't take long to decide it might not be a good idea either.

"Fine. You can pass," the voice called out.

I started pedaling and then stopped again, talking to the bush. "Just so you're aware, I'll be coming back this way *every* day. If you have different staff on at any point, please forward the information along to anyone in your employ so we can avoid an unfortunate misunderstanding."

"Sure. Now fuck off and get off the bridge. You're costing us money," the bush replied.

"I'm glad we are in agreement." I smiled and headed along, feeling a little cockier than I probably should've, but it was nice to be able to give these bullies the proverbial middle finger. It was nice to know I'd have insulin tomorrow and I had a bag of oranges tonight. It was just nice to have a day that went well for a change.

Chapter Seven

TIMMY WAS STANDING outside the door of the top floor of the apartment building, his red hair bright in the cloud of cigarette smoke haloing him.

He watched me approach, eyeing me up as if I were a filet, while he'd been eating hot dogs.

"I need to talk to Frank."

"You mean you want to request an audience?" he said, and then took a long drag from his cigarette.

As if this situation wasn't already unbelievable, Frank, the guy who used to work the fries at the local fast food chain, was establishing the proper etiquette for speaking to him.

"Yes. I need to request an audience with Frank." Even at the end of the world, certain things were just still too absurd. But Frank had become king of the building. If that was how the king liked things done, then that was how they'd be done, at least for now.

Timmy took another few drags of his cigarette, watching me for a minute. The pause was supposedly going to put me in my place and let me know I was so far down the totem pole I was barely visible. Timmy used to change oil for a living, but he'd gotten fired for forgetting to put the oil caps back on too many cars. Now he'd found the only job he was suited for: thug.

"Wait here and I'll see if he can squeeze you in for a few minutes."

I nodded, not bothering to ask what Frank was doing that made him so busy. I already knew. Him and his thugs had stolen all the solar panels in the neighborhood. This wasn't in an effort to get electricity and improve the living conditions of the building where he was king. No. It was so he and his merry gang of thugs could play video games. The top floor, where he and his men lived, also had use of the excess electricity for other creature comforts.

Timmy walked back out into the hall. "He'll see you for five minutes."

"Thank you." I tried to sound sincere, even as I was swallowing back bile.

The hallway was lit, with extensions cords lining the walls. The doors to all the apartments were open, and I followed the sound of video games.

Frank was reclining on a couch with his remote. Zombies walked around the screen of some apocalyptic game. Minus the zombies, it hit a little too close to home for me.

Seeing anything at all on a television screen drew my attention more than it would've a month ago. It was probably why it took longer than normal to notice the girl beside him. Her skirt was extremely short, heels ridiculously high, and she was sitting so close to Frank that she was nearly in his lap.

She tossed her hair back, glancing up at me. It was Eveline, the girl I'd seen the first night I went out scavenging. This couldn't have been her best option, could it? Maybe she'd run out of food, or been so lonely that even these people were preferable?

She looked away, as if she already hated me. For not bringing her here? Or because she was hating the world as a whole?

Roger, Frank's second-in-command, walked over to me.

"What's your visit about so I can relay the pertinent information to Frank?"

Frank, who was less than ten feet away from me, was acting as if I weren't there. I could handle the end of the world, but these antics might break me.

"I have my tax payment. I also want to move into a different unit." What I really wanted was to move into an entirely new place, nowhere near these people, but that wasn't feasible yet. It wasn't that there weren't plenty of properties available on the market, but I needed these idiots. They guarded the building when I had to leave Charlie and Widow Herbert. But if I could get a different unit, I could lock the door and keep my father from trading away everything I brought in for drugs.

"She wants to switch units," Roger said, as if Frank hadn't heard me.

Frank stopped hitting his remote for a second. "Not sure that's possible."

The majority of this building was empty and yet I couldn't switch? I had to pay these idiots and he wasn't going to let me move to one of the many open apartments?

"Frank says—"

"I *heard* him. Why?"

Roger turned toward Frank. "She'd like to know why?"

Frank finally got up from his seat, waving off Roger. Tucking his hands in his pockets, he grinned. "You have to understand that we have a list of people looking to move into a place with the type of round-the-clock security we provide. Most of the empty units are being negotiated for."

As unbelievable as that seemed, and by no means did I think every unit was taken, there was probably *some* demand. After all, why was I still here? Because they guarded the place.

"I've been living here since before Death Day. Don't you think I should get some preferential treatment?" I regretted the words as soon as I said them, knowing they'd open the door to a very bad conversation.

He smiled and moved in closer. "Some of the people moving in are offering sweeter deals. If you'd like, we could go in the other room and negotiate?" He wrapped his arm around my waist, tugging me toward a bedroom door.

I pulled back. "Aren't you already busy with one girl?" I motioned toward Eveline, who was glaring at me like I was the wife of Satan.

"She understands the ways of the world. Do you?" He closed the gap I'd just made.

I'd known he was going to make a move on me eventually and might be pushy about it. It was how pushy he might get that made me want to run out of there.

"I don't have time to negotiate anything right now. I have to go get to work. My boss Duncan over at News Blvd. will be upset if I'm late."

He stiffened. "You've got a job? With him?"

These shady types always did know about the bigger sharks in the pond. Before Death Day, name dropping was usually all about knowing celebrities. Now it was about knowing the meanest dudes on the block. It was probably what prison had been like. Now it was the mentality everywhere. It didn't bode well for the future of our species.

"Yes. He doesn't like when I'm late. He relies on me." I reached in my bag, pulling out the oranges. "Before I forget, here's your tax."

"Where'd you get these?" He was staring at them like I'd handed him a bag of diamonds.

"New boss. I think he's sweet on me," I said softly, like I was confiding a secret.

He took a step back. "I'll think about the apartment switch. Maybe there's something that can be arranged. I didn't realize you were uncomfortable. I want you to be happy here." He took another step back, as if he were worried he was crowding me.

"I'd really appreciate it."

He nodded, his face a little gray.

I headed for the exit. This situation could only go downhill from here.

Eveline was waiting for me by the door as I tried to escape, blocking my path.

"I know why you wouldn't bring me here, but it's too late now. He's mine, and you better stay away from him," she said. There wasn't a trace of tears left in those scheming eyes. She was clearly already cracking. She hadn't lasted long.

"I don't want your man. Now get the fuck out of my way before I knock you out." I'd never hit anyone in my life before the world had fallen apart. Now with the shiner, I looked a little scarier. Plus, I wasn't quite sure I *wouldn't* hit her. I'd about had it with people this week.

She moved out of my way, not so sure of me either.

Chapter Eight

I'D DROPPED off Charlie at Widow Herbert's, and I rode my bike to the back of Duncan's building and then left it close to the Hummer parked there. The truck had really fat tires that probably fared better than a lot of vehicles at this point. If no one stole that thing because they were afraid of the owners, hopefully that fear would carry over to my pink bike with the white wicker basket. They'd probably think it was their kid's or something, right? I moved it a little farther into the shadows, just to be on the safe side, before I walked into the building.

Rastin was sitting at a table in the middle of the place, with his back to the door.

"She's back," he yelled, as if alerting other people in the building that the plague had returned.

He raised his hand and waved me closer, still not looking at me.

I walked closer and stood beside the table. He lifted his finger, silently asking for a minute. Then he took at least three or four as I looked about the place.

They'd owned it prior to Death Day, hence the calling card. What had these people been doing here? Had they been mixed up in some sort of Mafia stuff? That was the weird kind of no-name vibe the place had. Pete had said they were bad news before he'd dropped dead. I wished I had dug a little deeper.

"Too bad Pete's dead. Very inconvenient," I mumbled as I looked around and then caught myself. What the hell was wrong with me?

"Who's Pete?" Rastin said, still looking at his books.

He was actively ignoring me, but *that* he had to acknowledge?

"A guy I know over at…" Yeah, that place was gone too. "A guy I knew. He made really good pizza. I didn't mean to sound glib. I liked him. He was nice."

Rastin leaned back, finally turning his full attention to me. "There were a lot of good people that aren't here anymore. You start crying over all the dead now and you'll never stop. Death Day happened, and now the ones left have to get on with living."

He shrugged, as if to say it was the way it was and to get over it. Unfortunately, he was probably right. That didn't mean I felt like having this conversation with him of all people.

"So what should I do?" I said, looking around the place. It wasn't like they had customers or anything.

Rastin looked at me, his nose wrinkling. "I'm not quite sure myself. You don't look very strong. I don't think it would do much good sending you out on most of the errands I need running. That might end up causing me more grief and work."

Whatever those errands were, I had a very strong hunch I didn't want to do them. If he was looking for some sort of enforcer, I wasn't it.

"I'm stronger than I look, but I do have my limitations." It wouldn't be good for him to get any crazy ideas about my roughing anyone up.

He let out a breath so hard his lips flapped as he looked around. "Maybe tidy up around here and just do... I don't know. Just go do something." He shooed me with his hand.

The place looked pretty tidy to begin with. Was he blind or trying to get rid of me? "And you'll pay me to clean?"

"Yeah, of course. We're not crooks." His face screwed up as if I'd tracked in dogshit.

"I'm only checking because the place looks pretty clean." The last thing I needed was to piss off my bosses the first day on the job. I already had enough issues going on.

He slumped back in his chair and shook his head. "I'm not sure you're fully understanding our situation here." He waved a finger back and forth in between us. "Duncan said to give you something to do, but I don't like managing people. I don't care what you get done. You could go take a nap and I'd happily pay you as long as you don't need anything from *me*." He paused, waiting for his words to sink in. "We understand each other now?"

"Yes." He might not care if I did anything, but the idea of napping? It was a little too awkward.

I took a step and stopped. "Where's your cleaning supplies?"

He looked up. "How would I know? Someone comes and does it. Just look around," he said, waving me off.

I glanced around the place. I was going to get paid to clean a place that wasn't dirty? Well, I wasn't going to argue with him. He clearly didn't care what I did, as long as it wasn't his problem.

I moved behind the bar, looking for rags or something. I

located some under a sink. Then I looked for something to clean and hit another wall.

I began wiping already clean surfaces while he remained bent over a book, grumbling. I kept it up for another ten minutes before I couldn't stand the idiocy of it anymore.

Yes, I'd thrust myself upon these people, but some scrap of dignity still wanted me to feel useful, like I wasn't being handed charity. I was going to contribute whether they wanted me to or not, and damn anyone who tried to stop me.

I walked over to Rastin again, stopping in front of his table. He looked up, his expression that of a four-year-old with a plate of lima beans in front of him. That painted me in a very unfortunate light, but they were paying me, so I'd be the worst vegetable ever if I needed.

"There is nothing to clean. You know, since you have cleaning people and all?"

"I don't care," he said. He was rolling his eyes, as if annoyed I'd pointed out this obvious fact and not gone along with his plan.

"What about that?" I pointed to his book. His hand had been poised over the same ledger page since I arrived.

"You want to help with the books?" His eyebrows shot up.

"Yes. I want to do something to earn a wage."

His smile lit, and suddenly this bad lima bean looked like a chocolate-covered marshmallow. He stood and motioned for me to take his seat. I picked up his pencil and scanned the page. There were lists of names, and items, either brought or taken. Seemed like a pretty clear-cut business for apocalyptic times.

"That stack of notes has to go into that book," he said.

"Okay, I got this."

"Really?" he asked.

"Yes. Really." He must really hate any kind of paperwork if he thought this was bad.

The toughest part of the bookkeeping was deciphering the chicken scratch. Whoever wrote some of these notes hadn't been overly concerned about being able to read them later.

Looked like Birdie had given a Julio Z. a five-gallon container filled with diesel gas. He'd also given this same Julio a bag of potatoes. Zach had brought in ten gallons of regular gas. I scanned the book for his name, figuring there must be some sort of debt he was repaying. Three pages back, he had borrowed five gallons. Not a bad return.

I flipped even farther back. Similar columns, names, and numbers, but the rest was written in code. Bookies? Gangsters of some sort? It wasn't like I hadn't been warned they were shady. It didn't matter anymore, though. The whole world had turned shady. At least these guys had some experience.

"Here," Rastin said, returning to the table and handing me a bag.

"What's this?" Was this bag stuffed with more notes? I might not finish this week if it was.

"Your pay for the day."

I looked inside, and it was filled with insulin, enough to last Charlie a month.

I hadn't cried when I was punched in the face, and yet now I was barely holding back tears.

"Who's it for?" Rastin said, watching me.

I debated lying for a minute, but these guys didn't care enough about any of my secrets to bother. "My little brother. He's only five."

He nodded and then walked into the back. He came back out with box he put on the table. "You can take these too."

Barry's Sugar-Free Chocolate Keto Bars.

"Thank you." I stashed it into my bag, trying not to do a double take. Since Death Day, survival had been a dirty battle, crawling through the muck that was left, every person still alive dropping to their lowest common denominator. Somehow getting this box of candies for Charlie was splitting me apart at the seams. I could feel the tears trying to break free.

"Okay, well, I gotta go," Rastin said, hightailing it toward the door like my watery eyes had set off an alarm. "If anyone comes, holler in the back. If no one is there then just tell them to come back tomorrow."

Chapter Nine

I WAS BIKING over the bridge on my way to work a week later when their leader stepped into the lane, waving for me to stop. They hadn't bothered me once since I'd told them I was working for Duncan. If they were going to ambush me now, it didn't seem logical that they'd give me a warning.

I slowed to a stop, but not so close he could grab me. This new world wasn't one where you could make careless mistakes.

"Did you need something?" I said.

"I wanted to talk to you for a few minutes if I could?" He was being awfully polite for someone in a leather jacket with metal studs, with a knife strapped to one leg and a gun to the other.

"Yeah, okay."

"I was wondering if you could talk to your boss for me?" He tilted his head to the side, almost bashfully.

"I, um…" Telling him I hadn't seen Duncan once since that first day might lower my chances of making it home. Telling him the guys almost completely ignored me other than handing me a bag of supplies at the end of my shift didn't seem so bright either. "You don't want to go yourself? It's not that far from here. Face to face can sometimes be better." I sounded like I was coaching him in sales or something.

He glanced over at the bushes, where his guys were probably hiding, and then took a few more steps toward me.

"I don't think he likes me much," he said, soft enough that his people would have a hard time overhearing. "Bad things happen to people he doesn't like. I was hoping, since I'm letting you pass without a problem, that you could put in a good word for me?"

"I'll get him the message you're looking to talk, but I can't guarantee he'll be open to it." Getting him the message was the best I could promise. If Mr. Ambush interpreted that to mean I'd deliver the message directly, it was on him. It was pretty hard to speak to someone I never saw.

"I'd appreciate it." He nodded as he headed back into the bushes.

I got to work a few minutes later, leaving my bike in the back. How was I supposed to get Duncan to speak to the ambush guy when he didn't speak to me?

Rastin and Buddie were having a conversation in the corner, and no one bothered to look my way as I walked in. They didn't even stir when the door opened. It was as if they knew it was me before I stepped in.

The truth was that they probably didn't care who was walking in. That was how it was when you were the lion of the jungle.

I settled in and went to work on updating the books, figuring I'd try to get Buddie at some point when he was alone. I'd had very few conversations with him either, but there was always something more approachable about him.

Maybe it was because every time Buddie gave me my pay, which was insulin and supplies, the bag always seemed stuffed to the gills. He could broach the topic with Duncan, then I'd have done what I'd promised.

Rastin got up and walked into the back.

Buddie got up next and was glancing my way, almost looking guilty.

Something was definitely niggling at him. Were they going to fire me or something?

"Hey, Buddie, do you have a minute?" I had to talk to him about Mr. Ambush, but I was beginning to wonder if I was going to have a bigger issue.

"Sure," he said. He smiled, and even that wasn't quite right, like the corners of his mouth were at half-mast.

Something was wrong, like I'd just gotten my sea legs and a hurricane was about to blow in and knock me on my ass. "Is something wrong?" I asked, Mr. Ambush no longer top of my list of priorities.

"We should probably talk," he said, motioning to the booth where all the big powwows seemed to happen. "Want to come sit for a second?"

I hated when people said shit like that. We *were* talking. Why didn't he just say, "I've got something crappy to tell you"? *Hey, you're going to really hate this, so brace yourself and take a seat so you don't faint and bang your head when you get the bad news.*

I sat, waiting while he walked over to the bar and grabbed a couple of glasses and a bottle of bourbon, or whisky. I wasn't sure which, and it didn't matter anyway. I hated the taste of all the amber liquors. The issue was he thought I was going to need it. Even hating it, I'd probably drink it down after he laid the crappy news on me.

He came back over, pouring us both a couple fingers and sliding a glass in my direction.

"I'm more of a 'take it off with an ax' type. If you don't mind, toss the butter knife back in the drawer and just hack it off already." I took a generous sip of the poison he'd poured, embracing the burn as I prepared myself.

"We're leaving."

Yeah, this was exactly the kind of news I hadn't wanted to hear. It was the worst-case-scenario. I felt like everything around me was scorched earth, and now this place, my only reliable source of food and medication for Charlie, was going to be gone too.

The blow hit so hard it left me breathless and without words. I sat there, somewhere between dumbfounded and panicked.

He was leaning forward. "Look, we'll set you up as best we can before we go. We don't want to leave you high and dry."

It didn't matter what they gave me now. Frank knowing I was working here was one of the only things that was keeping him at bay. Once Duncan and the guys left this area, Frank would eventually strong-arm his way in and take whatever I had. If I left, I'd be on my own and groups of strangers would steal it. It hadn't just been the supplies they'd given me but their influence I'd leveraged. Once they were gone, so was the power that their name yielded.

"Where are you going?" I asked, clinging to the tiniest glimmer of hope that maybe there was still a way out of this mess.

He looked down at his glass, taking a long sip before he said, "I can't say."

"Is there any way I could maybe…"

He wouldn't even tell me where he was going. What were the odds he'd take us with him? Not only me but my little brother, and an elderly woman to boot? Zilch. Nada. Negative number territory. Why even humiliate myself by pushing the topic and making us both uncomfortable when the answer was so brutally obvious?

"I would bring you if I could. There are things that I can't…" He flexed his fingers a couple times. "Look, it's just not possible."

I took the glass of poison and threw the remainder of its contents back in one shot. I had to force it to stay down, not sure if it was my body rejecting the liquid or the situation.

"Look, we're leaving you this place fully stocked with guns, food, and meds. I'll make sure you get a set of keys, and we won't tell anyone we're leaving. It'll buy you some time."

He knew how screwed I was. Somehow it made it worse—not that these people owed me anything. It didn't matter how he tried to ease the transition, either. I'd never be able to hold it. Not by myself. He could leave me a hundred guns. Once people realized they weren't coming back, and they would, I'd be a sitting duck. No matter what supplies I had, even if it was enough to form a gang of my own, no one looked at me and thought, *Yeah, now there's a badass I'd follow into hell.*

Rastin walked back in, took one look at me, and suddenly froze.

"You told her," he said, almost in an accusatory tone, as if they hadn't planned on giving me any warning at all. Would I have walked in one day and found a note?

"I had to," Buddie said. "I wasn't leaving her a note."

Yep. They'd been planning on hightailing it out and leaving me a fucking note. I grabbed the bottle of poison and refilled my glass.

"Look, we're leaving you all sorts of stuff," Rastin said, running a hand through his hair until some of it was standing on end. "It's not like we're walking out and leaving you with nothing. You'll be well stocked."

"For as long as I can hold it." I had no interest in playing pretend.

No one spoke at all for a few seconds. We all knew the truth.

"When are you leaving?" I asked. That date was more important than anything. If I could find somewhere safe to stash the supplies, maybe I'd have a chance. This place would get raided the second people figured out they were gone. I'd have to figure out how to get the stuff somewhere else without being seen. It felt like you couldn't walk out the door these days without people watching. I guess that was what happened when there was nothing else to do.

Rastin wouldn't meet my gaze, and I narrowed my stare on Buddie.

"When? I need to know how much time I have to prepare." I wasn't above begging to get my answer.

Buddie finished his drink, looking at his empty glass instead of looking at me. "Three days."

Three days? I had three days to prepare. It was better than one, but not by much. Still, if I could find a place and do four or five runs a day... People wouldn't know they were gone imme-diately, so I might be able to squeeze out another couple of days.

"Look, I'm sorry we can't take you," Buddie said.

"Nothing personal," Rastin said. "You're actually not half bad for a—"

Buddie coughed loudly.

"What? A woman?" I asked.

"Um, yeah, a woman," Rastin said.

I'd eavesdropped enough to hear him speaking of other women in pretty high esteem. Something wasn't quite fitting, but I had bigger issues than determining whether Rastin was a misogynist right now.

"We all have to do what's best for us. I get it."

I did understand. Why *would* they take me? I was dead weight. I wasn't going to beg for them to take me, either. Absolutely not. I'd make it on my own in this screwed-up world, one way or another. I'd have to make it, and I'd do it so well that Charlie wouldn't come out of this thing as scarred as I already was.

I took a few more sips of my poison and then stood with determination. "Can you show me what you're going to leave me? I need to start planning."

Buddie and Rastin looked at me with mirroring expressions, as if surprised I was handling this so well. If they could've seen the chaos inside me, they would've been running for the hills.

I spent the rest of my time writing down a list and then going over a map I'd found in one of the cabinets here. If I stashed different supplies at different places, it would buy me some time. They wouldn't find everything all at once.

I walked into Widow Herbert's unit with the key she'd given me a few hours later. Charlie was asleep on the couch. I nodded toward the kitchen.

"What is it?" she asked.

I sank into a chair, trying to keep the panic out of my voice. "They're leaving in three days."

"Where are they going?" she asked, looking concerned for the first time in all of this.

"They won't tell me, but they're leaving a bunch of supplies. I've got to find somewhere to move them, though."

She had her chin sitting on her fisted hand as she took it all in. "Frank and the other snakes will see if you bring too much here. You might as well hand them the stuff at the door."

"I know." I pulled the map out of my pocket. "I'm going to start scouting out places tomorrow."

She nodded silently, not offering any of the false platitudes I detested. We were screwed, and we both knew it.

Chapter Ten

MY BIKE TIRE WAS FLAT. I'd kept it together the entire time I was working tonight. I hadn't said a bad word or looked at anyone as if they were abandoning me, because I wasn't their problem. But now my tire was flat and everyone had left, and it felt all too similar to where I would be in a couple more days.

I knelt in the dirt, trying to figure out the issue, and a tear broke free. That single escapee felt like a prison riot, breaking open the gates for all his friends to follow. I was kneeling there, my forehead resting against the outside of the building, my shoulders shaking. I was so loud in my sobbing it took me a bit to realize Duncan was standing beside me.

I wasn't sure how many times he'd called my name before I heard him. I dragged my arm over my face and leaned back, trying to sound normal. Of all people, it had to be him that found me like this? The one who set my nerves on edge more than anyone? I hadn't seen him at all, and now here he was.

"Did you need something?" I asked, hoping I sounded

normal enough, as if he hadn't seen me here bawling over my bike.

"What are you doing?" he asked.

"Uh, I've got a flat. I'm trying to fix it." Or I was going to after my pity party closed for the night. Last call should be any day now.

He raised his brows. I wasn't sure if it was because he thought I was stupid or because I'd been obviously in the middle of a breakdown.

"What?" I asked, sounding as defensive as I felt.

"You can't stay here. Not tonight."

I stiffened, as if he'd thrown a slur my way.

"I not. I'm just going to see if I can fix my tire, and if I can't, I'll walk home. I'm not trying to stay here." He really couldn't wait to get rid of me.

He looked down toward the road, and then back, looking even edgier than normal.

"No. That's not going to work. You need to go now." He had a tone that assumed his every word would be given deference.

"I'm not trying to stay. I'm going to leave." If he made me tense, the reason was clear. He was acting as if I were an Ebola outbreak he wanted to flee. He was pushy and aggressive and all-around unlikeable. Even if he was attractive, it didn't make up for all the deficits in his personality, which were too many for any sane human to waste their time listing.

He was looking at me, and then he shook his head. I thought he was going to walk away, but he didn't. He took a step toward me.

"Get up."

"Huh?"

"Get up. You need to come inside."

I didn't move. I sat there, staring at him, frozen for a few seconds. "I'm going to be on my way in two seconds. You don't need to stay here and make sure I depart. Trust me, I'll leave willingly." It wasn't as if he knew how many times I'd imagined what life could be like if they just took me with them. Let me be part of the gang.

"I don't have time for this. You can't sit here. Get. Up."

Did he just growl? What was wrong with this man?

"No, I'm good. I swear."

He reached for me. I instinctively grabbed on to the nearest thing I could, which was a pipe that ran along the building. He grabbed my wrists, squeezing them, making my fingers go numb before he tossed me over his shoulder.

"What are you doing? You can't kill me." I tried to kick, but his grip around my legs was too tight. "People know where I am. They'll find you."

It was a joke. It was like telling the grizzly bear I was going to sic my pet chihuahua on him. He clearly agreed, because he didn't break his stride.

"Trust me. I'm not *stealing* you. I'm bringing you inside because you can't stay out here right now."

How his words were more insulting than getting lugged over his shoulder was a testament to how despicable he was.

"Just so you know, a lot of people would love to steal me," I said, still hanging over his shoulder.

He walked into the empty bar and then proceeded to the back, and then toward a door I'd never been through and up a flight of stairs.

I didn't ask if he was planning to ravage me, either. Clearly I wasn't up to his standards. I never thought I could be so offended by someone not attacking me, but there it was. I'd finally lost my mind with the rest of the world.

He put me down in a living room of sorts. I'd always wondered what was on the second story.

"I'll have your bike fixed in the morning. Don't leave these rooms until I come for you. Do not go downstairs, no matter what. Do you hear me?" he asked, his hand already on the door to leave. I was Little Miss Ebola after all.

"I don't know why I can't just walk home," I said, crossing my arms.

"Don't. Leave. If you hear something, don't look out the window," he said.

"I can't look out the window?" I squinted, feeling as if I couldn't have heard him correctly.

He leaned closer. "Don't look. Don't hear. Don't leave. You won't like what happens if you do."

"Okay. I hear you." I paused a second before adding, "Or don't I?" It was stupid and idiotic, and I didn't even know why I was trying to annoy him. Maybe I was still smarting over his rejection, or non-rejection, or everything about him.

He ignored my comment. I was too low to even be able to insult him.

"I'll be back in the morning," he said.

I'd told Widow Herbert I was going to be scouting out places tonight anyway, so it wasn't like she'd be worried. I would have the keys to this place soon. It might not be so bad to know what I was getting. He'd said I couldn't look outside. He hadn't said anything about inside.

It looked like a random apartment that wasn't being lived in. There wasn't a speck of dust, or a hint that anyone lived here. There were oil lamps all over this place too. I was going to have to ask them to leave a few, since they had some to spare. How good was their current living situation if no one stayed here? Where did they go? How nice was *that* place?

And how good was the place they were planning on going to? I'd never know, but maybe I could figure out a way to hole us all up here for a week or so before word got out?

I lit a few lamps, grabbed a home-decorating magazine that had a date that was only a couple of months old, and settled in. It wasn't exactly something pertinent to life now, but for just a little while, maybe I could pretend the world hadn't ended.

Chapter Eleven

THERE WAS a loud clattering noise outside my window.

Don't look. Don't hear. Don't leave. Those were the instructions I'd received. Pretty clear, and should've been easy to follow if you weren't the curious type, which *I* was. Still, this new world had burned some of that out of me. I guess that was what happened when every time I did look, I wished I hadn't.

I waited for another noise, if only to make sure I was safe and sound. When I didn't hear a thing, I went back to my magazine. Crisis averted. Box checked. I'd stayed within given orders.

I flipped another page to see a house with a beautiful atrium. Maybe when things eventually settled down, I'd find a house like that. Charlie and Widow Herbert would love it.

I was admiring the plants when I heard a groan. It seemed like it was coming from below the window nearest me. Maybe I was wrong. Maybe the wind was rubbing a couple branches together. It looked like a storm was coming.

Another groan. No, this wasn't two branches. Someone or something was in a whole hell of a lot of pain.

Don't look. Don't.

Would Duncan *really* know if I peeked?

There was another moan. Screw this.

I lowered all the lamp lights and crawled over to the edge of the window, pulling back the side of the drape a sliver.

The window was in the front of the building, with the porch roof right below. All I could see was a pair of boots sticking out, and the beginning of a man's legs. Another groan. Whoever it was, they were in a lot of pain.

The clouds moved past the moon, and I got a better view of black boots with a distinctive white tab on the side. I knew those boots.

This time it was me groaning.

Buddie. It was *Buddie* lying there.

Buddie, the one who'd been slipping me extra food. The person who'd been honest with me when I asked him what was going on. The rest of them had planned on leaving me a note, but he'd told me. Why couldn't it have been anyone else groaning down there?

I had to get closer. Maybe he was just drunk? I needed a better view. I ran to the door and realized that fucker Duncan had locked me in or blocked the door somehow. Damn him.

I went back to the window, pulling the drapes wide and trying to spy any possible threats. If his attacker was here, wouldn't he have come and finished the job?

I leaned out, calling as loud as I dared, "Buddie?"

A soft moan was all the response I got in return. It was the sound of someone in pain and definitely not drunk.

This was bad. *Really. Bad.* He might be dying. Why did it have to be the nice one? Rastin I might've been able to ignore. Duncan I definitely would have ignored. But it was Buddie.

Before I let myself think it through, I climbed out onto the roof, glad I had on sneakers that had a good grip as I shimmied closer to the ledge. I got on my belly and shimmied down until I was hanging and then dropped the last several feet down.

Buddie was lying there, conscious and looking at me, but his eyes were barely open, and his white shirt was now soaked red from his shoulder to his stomach. That he was awake was the most surprising part.

I dropped to my knees beside him. "What the hell happened?"

He tried to say something.

I leaned closer. "What?"

I scanned his body, realizing most of the blood was coming from his upper-right chest and finding a hole in his shirt. Someone had shot him.

"Inside," he said, trying to lift his hand and point in that direction. His arm barely left the porch.

He was right. I had to get him out of sight. We might leave a blood trail, but at least it would be a little harder if they had to break down a door. Just because I didn't see anyone didn't mean they weren't about to show up.

"Keys in pocket," he said.

I got the door open and looked at him. This wasn't going to be that easy, for either of us.

"You're too big for me to carry. I'm going to have to drag you in," I said.

He nodded. I didn't want to put any kind of pressure on his upper body, so I grabbed a handful of his jeans by each ankle. I'd known he'd be heavy by his size, but it was like trying to move a boulder.

He weighed even more than he looked like he would. I was winded after a few steps, and only desperation and adrenaline kept me going. It took me ten minutes to get him inside, and then I immediately locked the door and pulled down the shades.

I grabbed some rags from the bar and pressed them against the hole in his chest. That he was still alive with the amount of blood coming out of him was a miracle in itself.

I cupped his cheek with one hand. "Buddie, you gotta stay with me, okay?"

"There's a bullet. Dig it out." His eyes were open and he was staring at me, seeming so lucid.

"Duncan said he'll be back. He'll know what to do." I didn't know how to operate on anyone. If I did what he wanted, he'd be dead in minutes.

"You gotta get it out. I'll die if you don't."

"Trust me, you'll die if I do. Our best bet is for me to apply pressure to slow the bleeding until someone gets here." Someone who'd know what to do, which definitely wasn't me.

His hand, still lying limp, gripped my pants. "You don't understand. What they shot me with is what's killing me. Get the bullet out or I'm dead."

"Buddie, I need you to lie still." If he didn't stop using what strength he had left to stay alive, he'd really die fast.

"You have to or I'll die."

He was staring at me so intensely, it was hard to shake the fear that maybe he knew what he was talking about.

I looked at the door. Duncan might not be back for hours. Buddie wouldn't make it that long anyway. He'd be dead. It wasn't like I could call an ambulance or drive him to the hospital. I was it, and with the rate he was bleeding out, even with my putting pressure on it, was there really much of a difference if I tried to remove the bullet like he wanted me to?

"Piper, do it and I'll live. You have to do it."

Was he losing his mind? He seemed convinced. He might be dead either way. At least I could do what he'd asked for with his dying breath.

"Fine."

"Dig until you find the bullet. Get. It. Out." He was nearly growling, and I jerked back to look at him for a second, because it almost sounded as if he were possessed.

His eyelids were heavy, and pain streaked across his ashen face.

If I was going to do this, it had to happen now. He was going to be dead soon anyway with the amount of blood that was pouring through my fingers.

"Buddie, thank you for trying to help me." It might be the last chance I had to say that.

He nodded ever so slightly.

I took a deep breath, wrapping my mind around what I was about to do to his poor body, and then dug my fingers into him. I tried to follow the hole the bullet had made. His blood and flesh were warm and squishy against my fingers. I started off timid enough, but as the blood gushed out, it became very clear I didn't have the liberty of time. I had seconds, not minutes. The quicker I did this and got my hand out, the quicker I could go back to applying pressure and not kill him.

I dug in deeper, trying to follow the path of damage until my finger touched something hard. I pushed deeper, ignoring his moan of pain until I was able to get a grip on the bullet and pull it out of his chest.

"It's out," I yelled triumphantly. I grabbed the rags,

pressing them to his chest again, hoping I hadn't done irreparable damage.

He took in a deep, ragged breath that expanded his entire ribcage.

"Thank you," he said, exhaling as if I'd given him a shot of opium.

I nodded, keeping the rags in place as I leaned over and applied pressure. My head dropped forward, and my hair formed a curtain around my face as I tried to keep my shit together. I felt like a pressure valve wanting to shoot off, and I was either going to start crying or laughing hysterically any second.

He began to shudder under my hands. Oh no. He was dying. I'd stolen his last few minutes because I'd listened to the insane ramblings of a man with a mortal wound. What if I'd waited? Bought him some time?

I pressed firmer on the wound, trying to stanch the blood that had already slowed, probably because his heart was failing. A sob escaped as the pressure valve finally began to blow and I succumbed to tears.

I lifted the rags—the blood seemed to have ceased flowing —and sat back on my heels, doing the only thing left. I took his hand, gripping it between both of mine.

"I'm sorry, Buddie. I'm really sorry."

My vision blurred with the tears flowing. I held his hand to my chest, giving him the only thing left I could: the presence of another person at his side as he passed.

I was sobbing so hard that I didn't notice the change initially. Hadn't felt the difference in the hand I held until I felt something pointy against my skin. I swiped an arm across my eyes, trying to clear the blur of tears, and realized the hand I was holding wasn't human. It was something closer to what I'd find on a creature from my nightmares.

I dropped it with a shriek as my brain tried to make sense of it. Then I looked at Buddie. His entire body was changing in front of me. His torso expanded until the buttons of his shirt began to pop off and shoot across the room. I leaned away from him and then crawled back another few feet as he transformed into a monster that matched the hand I'd held.

For a few seconds, I couldn't scream or move. I sat there, frozen in shock. I had to get out of there. I had to leave this place before this thing woke up.

I got to my feet, slipping on the blood underfoot and then righting myself as I rushed toward the door.

It was swinging open, Birdie and Rastin blocking the way out.

They looked at Buddie, or the monster that had been Buddie, and the trail of blood. Then me.

"What the hell happened?" Rastin asked.

Chapter Twelve

"DON'T. MOVE," Rastin said, looking down at me where I was tucked into the corner booth.

I wrapped my arms around my legs and propped my chin up on my knee, eyeing them up as they took a seat at the nearest table.

Buddie was sitting up, back to looking human, his shirt hanging open and covered in blood. Were they all monsters? I wouldn't ask, but I had my suspicions. Right now I didn't want to be here, let alone speak to them.

"Let me get this out of the way. She saved me. I'm not letting anyone kill her," Buddie said. The monster then glanced my way with his friendliest smile, as if to reassure me he had my back. I swallowed hard. Well, at least the monster was grateful. That had to count for something.

Wait, why did he have to state that he wouldn't let them kill me? Why would killing me be on the table at all?

"How are we supposed to let her live? She saw you shift," Birdie said. He glanced my way. "Sorry. It's nothing personal.

I wouldn't vote to kill you under normal circumstances." Then he shrugged.

Was that supposed to help? *Nothing personal*?

"You'll have to get through me first," Buddie said.

At least he was a loyal monster. Not like Birdie, who probably gave all those horror movie monsters their bad names. *Dick*.

"It's your fault, Buddie. Why'd you have to keep giving her so much stuff? You made her keep coming back," Rastin said.

Yep. They were all monsters. I'd suspected, but that put the final nail in the coffin. Or the silver bullet in the beast? Stake in the vampire?

I felt like I couldn't get enough air into my lungs. *Don't hyperventilate*. If I looked like an unstable mental case, it would add one more mark in the Reasons to Kill Piper column. I'd read somewhere that I couldn't hyperventilate if I breathed through my nose. My nostrils were probably flaring out like I'd grown wings on my face.

"Like you didn't send her home with extra shit?" Buddie said.

"Yeah, but you were nicer. Now what the hell are we doing with her?" Rastin asked.

"I'm not letting you touch her. She saved me, and that's not the way we repay people," Buddie replied.

There was even more yelling between them, but I wasn't paying attention anymore, as something struck me. Duncan had felt indebted to me for helping out a relation of some sort. Now Buddie was mentioning the way they repaid people.

If backing a couple of kids off Duncan's relation had scored me all the resources I'd gotten over the last couple weeks, then what would be payment for saving Buddie's life?

A few months ago, looking for tit for tat wouldn't have been my thing, but today?

My adrenaline was cranking so fast and hard that I was nearly shaking as I slid out of the booth and came to stand in front of their table.

They all quieted down to stare at me, as if they'd sensed some sort of shift in a paradigm.

I looked each of them in the eye as I said, "I saved Buddie. I want to go with you, wherever you're going."

No one spoke. They just stared at me, as if I was the one who'd morphed into a monster.

"Well?" I said. "Doesn't that entitle me to some kind of request?" I knew in my gut that I was onto something.

They all looked at each other, as if afraid to be the one to speak.

They didn't have to. Their silence said it all. "It does. Doesn't it?"

"Where's Duncan? He's supposed to be here by now," Rastin said, shifting in his chair a little too actively.

Birdie got up, looking out the window.

"Just admit it," I said.

Buddie drummed his fingers on the table for a second and then said, "She's correct. I think we're going to have to take her."

"What the fuck, Buddie?" Rastin said. "She's not one of us. She's a human."

Oh yes, they were *all* monsters. I was trying to make a horde of monsters take me with them. Yet who would be better at the end of the world?

"Duncan is here," Birdie said.

"Good. Someone needs to put an end to this," Rastin said.

Duncan walked in and stopped, looking around the room,

from me, to Buddie's ripped and bloody clothing, to the blood still pooled on the floor. "What the hell happened?"

"I had a bad night and took a shot. I got here and Piper saved me. Now she's calling in the debt," Buddie explained.

Duncan turned his gaze toward me, and the force of his anger was so potent it felt like time was slowing.

"You weren't supposed to leave the apartment," he said.

"If I hadn't, Buddie would be dead." The nerves that usually made me all tangled up when he spoke to me seemed to be smothered by shock, anger of my own, or maybe the death threats. It was hard to know.

He turned to Buddie. "Is this true?"

"Yes. Now she's asking for repayment. She wants to go with us." Buddie smiled in some sort of perverse form of apology.

Duncan looked at me with barely concealed distaste at the thought of bringing me along. Was he going to tell them to kill me? Why did this guy hate me?

"Hope you're packed, because we aren't waiting on you," he said.

What? I wasn't the only person floored. There were gasps coming from the table.

"Seriously? We have to honor this? She's not even a shifter," Rastin said, on his feet.

"We honor our debts. It doesn't matter who or what she is," Duncan said. His gaze glided over me again, and then he walked to the back.

"But she's got a kid!" Rastin yelled after him.

Duncan paused. "Then go get the kid and get it handled tonight. I've decided we should leave tomorrow. Now, if that's it, I have a lot to do before we make the trip." He left the room.

Rastin walked closer. "I'm not sure you realize what you're asking for."

"Whatever it is, it's better than staying here," I said, digging in. I didn't care if they were bringing me to hell with them at this point. Staying behind meant certain death for Charlie, because I'd never be able to keep a supply of insulin for him.

Chapter Thirteen

RASTIN WALKED to the door and looked at me. "Let's go."

"Now? You want to get my brother right now?" I'd thought I'd have some time to think about this, make sure I wasn't insane, and come to terms with the decision. I'd thought there would be a chance to warn Charlie and Widow Herbert of what we were going to do. They didn't even know she was coming yet.

"Come on." Buddie was making his way to the door.

I headed toward my bike. My tire was still flat.

"We're taking the Hummer," Buddie said.

I grabbed the bike, carrying it toward the vehicle.

"What are you doing?" Rastin asked, not opening the trunk.

Buddie grabbed it and put it back alongside the building. "Worry about that later," he said.

I didn't like leaving my bike anywhere. I was still staring at it when Duncan walked out of the building.

"I'm going to ride with you guys," he said, hopping in the passenger seat.

What? It was one thing to surprise Rastin and Buddie with Widow Herbert, but now Duncan would be there too? It wasn't like I could tell him he couldn't come.

"Get in," Buddie said.

I hadn't realized he'd been standing by the door, waiting for me. They were all staring, each looking more annoyed than the next.

I climbed into the truck.

"What about the roads?" I asked.

"We know what routes are clear enough for us to get by," Buddie said.

"Clear enough" meant they could drive over cars left in the road. I wasn't going to think about what was also in those cars.

Everywhere we went, we drew eyes because no one was driving these days. If they were, they weren't driving anything that needed much gas. Along with food, medicine, and everything else, these guys must have a stash of gasoline a river deep.

"You need to turn left up there. I live over by south—"

"We know where you live," Rastin said.

They knew where I lived, like the exact address, not just vicinity. This day just kept getting creepier and creepier.

We rode in silence as I wondered what was going to happen when we got there and they found out we were picking up *two* more people. I was looking out the window, growing tenser and more rigid by the mile.

Buddie, who was sitting on my left, looked over and smiled, as if to assure me that everything would be all right. He was oblivious to how he appeared, his shirt torn and covered in so much blood that he'd put a stuck pig to shame.

Looking at him was making my anxiety worse. I looked back out the window.

We pulled up to my building and all piled out together, like some misfit commando unit.

Timmy was at the front door, signaling to get reinforcements on his walkie-talkie before we'd even hit the sidewalk. We were all going to get shot. I'd probably get hit accidently as they aimed for my companions. It wouldn't hurt any less because it was a mistake. Dead was dead.

These monsters would probably walk away unscathed, just like my messy friend Buddie. What would've killed anyone else was just a bad evening to him, a blip, like a bug in his Happy Meal.

We had only taken a handful of steps when I was pushed behind a wall of monsters, nearly obstructing my view completely.

"What do you want? Why do you have Piper with you?" Timmy asked.

I wriggled through the mass of muscle enough to see there were now four of our guards at the door, guns aimed at the chests of every male around me. Frank was just arriving. I could see the recognition, and then panic that shot into his gaze as he looked at Duncan. He buried it fast as his men looked to him for directions. This idiot was going to stand his ground to not lose face in front of his men.

"Frank, I'm just here to—" A hand on the waist of my jeans tugged me back behind them again.

"We're not looking for trouble, but we are going to her apartment," Duncan said.

"I know who you people think you are, but no one comes in here without my say-so," Frank said. "Now I suggest you turn yourselves around before you need to be carried away."

"We're trying to do this the easy way, mostly because I don't want to be bothered," Duncan said. It wasn't bluster, or a threat. He sounded as if he wasn't in the mood to swat away an annoying gnat.

I wasn't sure what was happening because I couldn't see past the male backs forming a wall in front of me, and no one was speaking. It couldn't be good, because there was a low growl humming all around me. If I had an opportunity to run, I would take it, and I wasn't even the target.

Several shots were fired and there was a flurry of movement. In a couple of seconds, Frank, Timmy, and the others were lying on the ground, unconscious.

"Are they dead?" I didn't like them, but still…

"Just taking a nap," Duncan said.

There was a gash on his neck, as if he'd been grazed by a bullet. It was closing up as I watched.

So now it was confirmed. I was surrounded by monsters.

"Buddie, go with her," Duncan said. "Be quick about it. I have other things I need to do tonight."

I headed for Widow Herbert's place. I was still trying to sort out how I was going to slip another person past them when I noticed how dirty and dingy the place had gotten. I'd grown almost blind to it until I caught Buddie looking at the trash piled up in the hallway.

Widow Herbert opened the door, smiling as she took in Buddie. "Oh, you've brought company! How nice! You know I love company."

I stepped into the apartment, and Buddie followed. I had to get her packed up and out of here before Buddie had a chance to come to his senses and stop me.

Charlie was in the living room, playing with his train set. He turned and let out a yelp as he ran to me.

"You're home early!" he said. "I can't go. I haven't fixed the clocks yet."

"Charlie, start putting your things in a bag. We're going on a trip."

Widow Herbert was smiling, looking like she was an elderly lady off her rocker as she took in everything going on.

"Where are we going?" Charlie asked.

I knelt beside him. "We're going to go stay with my new friends for a while. They're very nice."

"Is Daddy going to come with us too?"

"He might follow us a little while later," I said, not feeling even a little guilty about the lie. He was too little for the full truth. At some point there was no shielding him from the hurt, but for now I'd try.

I waited, praying there wouldn't be tears and not sure what I'd do if there were. We didn't have a choice. We had to go with them. I'd protect him with my life, but nothing was stopping this.

"Can I bring Graham?" he asked, not looking like he was going to have a breakdown, or cry, or even blink an eye at the change in plans.

"Of course you can bring him. Now pack up your bag, okay?"

He grabbed his bear and smiled. "Okay."

"Just need a second," I said to Buddie. I turned toward Widow Herbert, grabbing her arm and pulling her with me toward her bedroom.

The second I got her in the bedroom, I said, "Grab your things. We're moving, but we have to go now."

"Are we really leaving? You found us a new home?" Her face lit up like I'd promised her the Fountain of Youth.

"Piper, what are you doing?" Buddie yelled from the living room.

"We'll be out in a second!" I yelled back. If I could save his life, he could save Widow Herbert. "Yes, and with even better protection than this place," I told her. "Where's your suitcase?"

She pointed to the closet as she moved to her drawers. I helped her dump her things in.

"This everything you need?" I asked.

"One more thing." She walked to her nightstand, grabbed a picture of her late husband, and laid it on top. "I can't leave Walter alone."

"Piper? What's going on?" Buddie yelled from the other room, still staying out of the bedroom, as if afraid of what he'd find if he came in.

"Don't worry! Almost done!" I gripped Widow Herbert's hands. "You need to know something before we go."

"What?" she asked. Her voice was nearly breathless with anticipation. She'd told me in her youth she'd been a little bit of an adrenaline junkie. I was wondering if that might've been an understatement.

"The people we're going with, they aren't quite..." *Shit.* There was no nice way to say this. "They're monsters, and I don't mean that figuratively. Like, they aren't bad people. Actually, some of them seem halfway decent. When I say monsters, I mean *literally*. I saw one change, and it was scary as fuck. My lungs didn't inflate for a good ten minutes, and I'm surprised my heart is still beating. Please believe me. I'm. Not. Exaggerating."

I waited for her to freak out. To call me crazy.

She was too calm. She was almost always calm, like age had granted her this superpower.

"Okay, let's go." She turned to the door, and I jumped in front of her.

"I need to know you understand what you're getting into." Leaving here with them was definitely a leap of faith.

"I understand. They're monsters. But you like them, right?" She grinned.

"At least one of them. They seem to have some moral fiber and principles." They weren't all utterly heartless. That was something.

"Good. Let's go." She waved at the door.

She'd been warned, and it wasn't like I could leave her behind. I grabbed her bag.

Buddie was shaking his head at me when we appeared again.

"Piper, what the hell are you doing?" He looked directly at Widow Herbert.

"It'll be fine. She won't be a bother. She's tougher than she looks." I shuffled her toward the door, waving Charlie over as I did, feeling like I was trying to herd cats past a wolf.

"This is not going to go over well," Buddie said, sighing. But he was moving toward the door with us.

I grabbed Charlie's hand, and we walked out of the apartment like a gang of misfits.

"I am pretty scary looking, though, right?" Buddie asked softly as we entered the hall.

How much of my conversation had he heard?

"Incredibly so," I said. "Did you hear everything?"

His chest puffed up. "We've got really good hearing. The guys try to tell me my beast form isn't all that, but I know they're being jackasses. I'm every bit as scary looking as the rest of them. They don't want to admit it."

The other ones were worse? I hoped I never saw them shift. Ever.

"So your friends also shift?" Widow Herbert asked. "That's so nice for you all."

I tried not to look at her as she spoke. I didn't want to give up how absurd she sounded. What kind of game was she playing?

"Thank you," Buddie said, as if this were a normal conversation.

"Well, even though I've yet to meet them, I have little doubt that you hold your own amongst even the scariest. I was a psychologist for several decades. I could tell at first glance you were made of stern stuff," she said, smiling and then laying her hand on his arm. "My, you're very large."

Buddie's chest inflated a little more. "You know, no one in my pack ever says anything nice to me."

"They might feel intimidated by your abilities and ease with people. It's natural for others to be jealous of someone such as yourself."

"I've got to run upstairs for a few minutes," I said as we got close to the stairs. Widow Herbert was nodding, understanding in her eyes.

"Why?" Buddie asked.

"We need to say goodbye to our father." I didn't want to bring Charlie with me, but he deserved the opportunity to say goodbye. If it was only me, I wasn't sure I would've gone upstairs at all.

"He's alive?" Buddie asked, looking at Charlie, clearly trying to put the pieces together of why I seemed to be the one working for insulin and food.

"Yes. We'll be right back." I grabbed Charlie's hand.

"Should I come with you?" Buddie called, waiting with Widow Herbert.

"No. I'll only be a few minutes." I'd rather no one else have to see the condition I'd find Dad in. It was bad enough that Charlie would have to see him.

"So tell me more about this monster form of yours?" Widow Herbert said. "I bet it's absolutely ferocious."

Poor Charlie got tugged up the flights of stairs. Was I an idiot for bringing him with me? I could've run up and grabbed the few things I needed alone. But it was his father too.

My father was asleep on the couch, snoring.

"Dad."

He didn't stir.

"Dad!"

He jerked, opening his eyes.

"We came to say goodbye."

It took him two tries to right himself on the couch. "What? What do you mean? Where are you going? You're leaving?

"I'm not staying here, and I can't leave Charlie with you." I held back saying that if I did, Charlie would be dead in a week. My father wouldn't get off the couch to feed himself, let alone do what it took to get Charlie food or insulin.

"But where are you going?" He was scratching his face, and then his chest.

"Out of the city, a place with fewer people, more room. I'll get a message back to you somehow, letting you know where to go if you want to come." I wasn't sure if I said that for my father or Charlie. I certainly didn't believe it would ever happen. He'd die of an overdose in this apartment. Maybe in a week, or a month. I couldn't guess how long it would take, but it would happen.

"But how will you work there and get things? You'll be leaving your job."

"I'll manage."

He started crying, and then I watched as his wheels started turning. Reality was setting in. With me stuck here, he had a constant supply of items he could take to trade for drugs. Once I was gone, he'd have to do something other than get high.

"You can't take my son. He's mine. Not yours."

He knew I'd never leave Charlie. He thought he was going to keep me here, stuck. That I'd never get up and leave with Charlie. I'd known this moment was going to come, knew it was going to be ugly.

I shouldn't have come here to say goodbye. This had been a colossal mistake, some misguided notion of mine that it would be better for Charlie to see his father before he went. Now Charlie was clinging to my side like I'd walked him into hell.

"Charlie, say bye."

My father got off the couch and slammed me against the wall, bony hands wrapped around both my arms, pinning me there.

"You're not taking him," he said.

Charlie was crying and tugging at Dad's shirt.

"I won't stay to keep you supplied," I said. "Look what you're doing to him. Look what's become of you."

It didn't matter what I said. His eyes were glazed over, and there was no one left inside who cared. There was only one thing he wanted, and it wasn't his children.

"What about me? I'm doing my best."

I couldn't tell if he really believed that on some level or if it was all a scam to keep the situation going. I didn't care. We all had our own demons to fight, and I was learning fast that no one could take on that fight for us. We were each on our own, with our own battles to wage.

"We're leaving. Let go."

"You aren't taking him."

"Yes, I am."

Charlie was clinging to my leg, as if afraid I'd leave him here.

The door opened, and Duncan appeared inside the apartment. He wrapped his hand around my father's shirt collar, lifting him to his toes.

"You can either go sit on the couch and say goodbye nicely, or I can make you sit on the couch and we'll see if you can speak around all the broken teeth."

He let him go, and my father stumbled backward. Duncan took a step forward.

Dad backed up to the couch, sitting. "I was only—"

"I know what you were doing," Duncan said, dismissing him and looking at me, then Charlie. "Do you need anything else?"

"No." I grabbed Charlie's hand.

Duncan stepped back, motioning for me to leave first.

"Bye, Daddy." Charlie gave our father the briefest wave as we walked out.

He seemed all too eager to leave. He was leaving his father, not knowing when he'd see him again, and yet he didn't even attempt to hug him. There was something very unsettling about that, but I wasn't going to dwell on it now. I'd take it as a gift.

Charlie walked in between Duncan and me. He reached up and grabbed hold of two of Duncan's fingers—his hand was too little to wrap around them all.

Duncan had never shown himself to be cruel, but I couldn't quite breathe while I waited to see if he'd yank his hand away.

He glanced down at Charlie, who stared up at him as if he were going to be his new best friend.

"I'm Charlie."

Duncan squinted and then said, "Duncan."

I could see Charlie's face light up, as if the exchanging of names had just cemented their friendship.

Chapter Fourteen

"WHY ARE they lying on the ground?" Charlie asked as we walked out of the building.

"They're taking a nap." I ignored Duncan's look, as if I shouldn't lie to a five-year-old.

His attention was quickly diverted to Buddie, Rastin, and Widow Herbert standing in front of the massive Hummer.

"We get to go in that?" Charlie's little mouth gaped open as he looked at the huge truck. The kid had loved big cars from the moment he came out of the womb.

"Yes." I tightened my grip as we got close, noticing the way Buddie and Rastin looked to be having words.

"She's coming," Buddie was saying to Rastin as we neared. He seemed more determined to get Widow Herbert in the Hummer than me. I had to really give this flattery stuff a try.

"Old lady, I'd think about it if I were you," Rastin said.

Widow Herbert slammed down her cane, eyeing him up.

Where had that cane come from?

"Listen here, laddie," she said. "I'm ninety-six years old.

I've outlived everyone in my family, including my grandchildren as of last month. If you think you're going to scare me off, you're wrong. So shove over and make room."

Buddie picked up Widow Herbert and deposited her into the back of the Hummer before Rastin could say another word.

He handed Charlie up then. Duncan raised a brow as I pushed past him, getting into the Hummer next.

"I don't want them to be scared," I said.

"That doesn't seem to be a problem," he said.

I thought Buddie would follow me into the back, but Duncan did.

It took me longer than it should've to realize we weren't headed back to the bar. I might've noticed sooner if I didn't have Duncan's hard thigh pressed against mine, or his arm along the back of the seat behind me. The fact that I could barely focus on anything beyond where we touched was concerning. I only had time for one man in my life, and he was five.

I forced my attention to the neighborhood. It was one of the last industrial areas left, and the buildings all loomed like quiet, lumbering ghosts now.

The truck turned into the drive of one of the largest buildings. Rastin pulled up to a barbed-wired fence then typed into a keypad, and the gates opened on their own.

Did they have electricity? Like hard-wired? Not some hodgepodge of solar panels bubblegummed together?

I looked beyond the gate to the building and saw lights coming from within that didn't flicker and weren't warm, like they would be from oil lamps. The garage door opened and lights flooded the place. They didn't just have juice, they were *swimming* in it. The garage under the building was packed with trucks and cars of all sorts.

"Duncan, where do you want them?" Buddie asked as we all climbed out. Charlie was already running over to scope out some monster trucks.

"Twelve, where they'll be out of the way," Duncan said. "Figure out what they need tonight. I want to leave tomorrow morning."

"Make sure you don't overdo it," Rastin said. "I'm not a pack mule."

He turned to walk away, but not before Widow Herbert whacked him in the leg with her cane.

Rastin spun around, growling.

She shrugged. "Sorry, laddie. Cataracts and all. Can't see where I'm walking all the time."

So the cane wasn't so much a walking aid but a disguised weapon? Now it made sense.

Rastin turned to Buddie. "You better talk to her before we leave," he said, but he wasn't looking at Widow Herbert. He was motioning to me.

"I know." Buddie nodded and then waved his hand toward us. "Come on."

He ushered us toward an elevator. A month ago, I wouldn't have thought a thing about getting on one of these things, and now it felt like a deathtrap. I got on anyway, not wanting to highlight Widow Herbert's age or Charlie's youth as they climbed twelve flights of stairs. Until we got on the road tomorrow, I wouldn't do a thing to draw attention to the liabilities in our group.

"I thought we weren't allowed on these anymore?" Charlie said as the elevator took us up.

"This time is okay," I said, praying he'd shut up.

His nose crinkled as if it didn't make sense, but he let it go.

Buddie walked us down the hall, pushing open a door at

the end of the hall. "You'll stay here for tonight until we leave in the morning."

He hit the switch on the wall, and the place lit up. It was roomy and had walls that didn't reach the ceiling, as if it had been retrofitted. There was a living area in the center, a kitchen set up in the corner, and it looked like a couple of bedrooms and a bathroom off to the side.

"I'll be back in a few to take you down to pick out the supplies for the trip," Buddie said.

I immediately headed over to the sink, where Widow Herbert was standing.

"You think it works?" I asked, almost afraid to try it.

"We can't just stare at it," Widow Herbert said. She turned the knob on the hot water and then waited to see if it worked.

She let out an excited yelp a few seconds later. I ran my hand under it and then let out the same excited squeal. Did this mean we could get a hot shower? It had been weeks at this point.

"Is this where we're going to live now?" Charlie asked.

"No. We're just stopping here overnight. It's going to be safer out of the city." At least, I hoped, because it was going to be hard to leave hot water.

"Life is going to be different for a long time," Widow Herbert said, turning the water off. "We're going to need to have land to farm, and a place to raise animals. This isn't the place to be."

"Are we going to have cows?" Charlie asked, just as there was a knock at the door.

Buddie glanced at Charlie and Widow Herbert before settling his eyes on me. "It's probably better if I bring you down for supplies alone."

Back at the apartment building, I'd been able to shield

Charlie for the most part. Those days would be coming to an end, but I'd go down fighting.

"Can you watch Charlie for a few?" I asked Widow Herbert.

"Take your time. I'm going to go take a long, hot bath as soon as he falls asleep." She yawned and eyed up the couch.

"I wanted to talk to you before we left," Buddie said as soon as we were alone. "You need to understand something before we go. Our kind don't always like humans. It's not going to be easy. They'll let you stay and honor my request because Duncan has a lot of pull, along with some other things, but that only means that they'll tolerate you."

"What about Charlie?" I could take whatever they dished out, but if they bothered him? That was a hard line.

"He's a youth. Children tend to get a pass. They won't target an elder, either," he said.

I couldn't help but laugh. "I've got news for you. Widow Herbert is like a hundred-year-old piece of jerky. Tougher than you'd expect. I'm more concerned about what she'll do to someone else. But if someone messes with Charlie, I *will* kill them."

He laughed. "Hopefully you won't have to kill anyone."

"As long as they don't bother him, it won't come to that."

I didn't care how they treated me. This was my only shot to get Charlie somewhere better and out of the city. If it was just me he was worried about, it didn't matter. Here? We were sitting ducks. Whatever I managed to accrue would get stolen.

"What about you?" Buddie asked.

"What's better for him will be better for me, too. Let's face it, if you guys are worried about staying here, how do you think I'll fare?" I asked as we stepped onto the elevator.

He snorted. "Valid point."

We hit the third floor, and as soon as we got off the elevator, a leggy redhead strode toward us.

"And here comes trouble," Buddie said loud enough that the woman heard.

She laughed as she walked over. The chemistry between the two of them nearly scorched me.

"Piper, this is Allie, Duncan's sister."

She nodded in my direction, not altogether pleasantly, but she wasn't clawing my eyes out, either.

Something changed in her expression. "Wait, are you the roller-skating girl?"

"You mean from the roller rink?" How did this stranger know about me?

"Yes," Buddie answered for me.

She nodded, her gaze softening. "Thank you. That was my son you helped."

"Oh, yeah, of course. It was nothing." It was the last reaction I'd been expecting. "I hope he's doing well?"

There was a visible flinch, and then she nodded. My gut twisted as silence filled the air.

"We're heading out tomorrow," Buddie said, pushing the conversation along.

Allie seemed to jerk back into the moment. She looked at Buddie. "I know. Duncan told me. Well, safe travels," she said, the smile she'd given him before wiped from her face. She got on the elevator we'd abandoned as if she couldn't wait to get away from us.

"Her son was one of the ones we lost on Death Day," Buddie said.

Oh. Shit. I should've guessed from that pain that had flashed in her eyes. It had taken over her entire body.

"Come on. Let's get you packed up." He tilted his head, motioning down the hall.

The place was quiet, but there was a sense there were people behind these closed doors as we walked. He punched a code into a locked door and then flipped on the lights. There were rows and rows of shelving, all piled high with food, clothing, hygiene products—everything.

He held up a backpack, and not the kind I'd have taken to school. This was like a legit, "I'm going into the wilderness" kind of thing. He unzipped it and then handed it to me.

"How long will we be traveling?" I asked.

"A week, give or take. Depends on the conditions and luck."

I had a hunch the conditions were partially their new traveling companions.

He started walking down the aisles.

"Where are we going?" I asked. The only thing I'd cared about before was going *with* them. Now that was accomplished, a destination might be a smart thing to find out. I'd assumed it was out of the city, but now I wasn't certain he'd specified. "Are we heading south?" A longer growing season would be a plus.

"We're heading into the heartland, where there are more of our people. There's a pack out there that's better set up to thrive in a situation like this." He was scanning the shelves, searching for something.

"So they have a compound or something?" These were definitely questions I should've covered before naming my price for saving him.

"They're completely off the grid and self-sustaining."

That really left a wide range of living conditions. Still, I didn't want to be left behind, so did it matter? Nope.

"Ah! Socks," he said, throwing some in the pack. "These are wool. Much better if they get wet. I put enough in for all of you."

"What about Charlie's insulin? I have to carry his insulin."

"We've got some more in the fridge, but let's leave it cold until the last moment."

I nodded.

He started chucking more things into my pack, only hesitating now and then to check if it was getting too heavy.

"Hey, what about food? We haven't packed much." My bag was nearly filled.

"We'll hunt as we go." He nodded and winked, knowing exactly what I was thinking.

"How many people are going?"

"There are about a couple hundred of us spread out in this area, but only our small group is going." He was feeling up the fabric on a fleece as he answered.

"This place is amazing. Is that why only you guys are going? Everyone else would rather stay?" To be truthful, I was having my doubts on whether leaving this spot was smart. The amount of supplies they had here would easily get us through a year or so.

"We're leaving without them to scout out the route and logistics, but everyone will be coming eventually. Duncan doesn't think the city is the place to be with all the unknowns. There's a power vacuum right now. We need to consolidate before anyone makes any big moves. The chess game is in full swing, and it's easier to let them pick each other off here and then see who's left." He shook out a shirt, then held it up to his chest.

"Who are these people you're talking about? Other packs? Is that how you got shot? People making moves?" I asked, immediately regretting how many questions I'd asked him as he stopped clothes shopping and looked at me.

"We should probably save this conversation for another time," he said. "You should be set."

I cursed myself for overdoing it as we walked back into the hall.

A few more people passed us, eyeing me up as if they were trying to piece together what I was doing there. No one seemed to dare ask Buddie as they nodded to him. I was getting the impression that Buddie was pretty high-ranking in this crowd.

Charlie was fast asleep in one of the bedrooms when I got back to the suite.

"We all set?" Widow Herbert asked.

"As set as we can be. Buddie said they don't like humans much where we'll be going, but they'll go easy on Charlie." I left out the part about them cutting the elderly some slack. I settled down on the couch and saw two cups of tea waiting. "Is this for me?"

"Yes. Might be a little lukewarm by now."

"Thank you. I don't care." I curled my legs up, wishing I could stay in this little corner for the rest of my life.

"You know, they're a fine-looking bunch of men, especially that Duncan," Widow Herbert said, smirking over the rim of her cup.

"You do remember my telling you about the whole monster thing, right?"

She shrugged. "Times aren't like they used to be. We have to deal with the reality we have, not the one we want. You could do worse than hitching your wagon to one of those men."

She kept calling them "men," and that wasn't what they were. It didn't matter anyway. That wasn't a discussion I was willing to entertain tonight, tomorrow, or ever, considering they weren't even the same species as me.

"Just because the world has gone to hell, I'm not completely willing to jump into the dark ages."

"Well, the problem I'm seeing is not that you need a man, but you need *something*, whether it be guns, a tank, some attack dogs..." She threw a hand up. "Since you don't have any of *those* things, one of these men will do, and won't be much of a hardship either. A year ago, things were different. Now? Rough edges are a plus. If I were a little younger, I know where I'd be hitching my wagon. No one can be an island unto themselves right now."

"Can I worry about picking out a monster tomorrow and enjoy our few minutes of peace before we leave tomorrow?" I had a feeling this calm wasn't going to last long.

"I thought picking out who would be the best monster to bed would be enjoyable chitchat, but if you want to drink tea in silence..." She shrugged.

I didn't respond.

"And for the record, I would pick Duncan," she added a few minutes later. "What a body on that one. Although none of them are slackers in that department. You think it's those monster genes? I bet it is."

She made a humming noise, and I couldn't stop myself from laughing.

Chapter Fifteen

BUDDIE WAS at the door the next morning. "Are you ready?"

Yesterday I discovered real-life monsters, then I'd been squirreled away to their den. Today, for the first time since Death Day, I hadn't woken up in a state of panic. That had to mean something, right?

"Yeah," I said, trying to convince myself this was the right course.

Widow Herbert grabbed Charlie's hand, and we all made our way out of the building. There were more people around than there had been last night, and lots of people checking us out. From the expressions I caught, we definitely weren't welcome. It didn't bode well for the place we were headed, either.

"We're going in them?" Charlie was jumping up and down as he saw the two monster trucks waiting in front of the building. Rastin, Birdie, and Duncan were already out there, looking over a map. Gotta admit, seeing monsters standing in front of those trucks had me suppressing a grin.

"You bet, little man," Buddie said. "Which one you want to ride in? The yellow or the red one?"

"Red," Charlie said, pointing.

They looked like they came from some auto show, but it was the only way we'd make it over the cars littering the roads.

Buddie jumped up onto the back bumper of the red one, and Rastin came over, tossing up packs.

"We need to get the insulin," I said.

"Already packed," Buddie called as he rearranged bags.

I would've preferred to have seen it with my own eyes, but if he said he had it, he had it.

Birdie and Duncan were loading up the other truck as another man walked out of the building. His hair was wilder than Buddie's, but it couldn't compete with the glint in his eyes, like he was a feral animal roaming his territory.

"That's Trevor. He's coming, too," Buddie said.

I stared at him, feeling like I'd seen him before. Damned if I could place him, though.

He walked over to Buddie and Rastin, but not before nodding in my direction, as if he knew exactly who I was.

"Do I know you? I feel like I've met you, but I'm sorry, I can't remember when," I said.

"Yeah, on the bridge. I shot the guy running at you." He smiled and then pretended to have a shootout with his hands, like a little kid might.

"That was *you*?"

"Yep. I'm going to miss screwing with them on Wednesdays." He let out a deep laugh, adding to the crazy air he had.

"One of Trevor's favorite pastimes is acting like an unsuspecting victim, and then…" Buddie glanced at Charlie. "Doing not-pleasant things. He *really* enjoys it."

"I do," Trevor said. "I'm going to go get the gas jugs. You never know when we'll need a little extra to torch something." He was the only one laughing at his joke as he walked back into the garage.

I glanced over at Rastin and Buddie. "Is he, uh, you know…" I'd barely gotten myself invited on this trip. Calling their friend names might be ill-advised.

"Crazy?" Rastin offered.

"Trevor doesn't like the C-word, so be cautious," Buddie said.

Widow Herbert gave a slight shake of her head, as if saying, *I don't want to mess with that one.* I didn't need a degree in psychology to figure that one out. So I was traveling with monsters *and* a lunatic to boot.

"Are we taking one of the bridges over?" Widow Herbert asked.

"No. Bridges were blown up," Duncan said.

I jumped, not realizing how close Duncan had gotten.

"Then the tunnels?" I said, trying to act as if his presence didn't unsettle me. Or how close he was now standing. Didn't these people believe in personal space? The sleeve of his shirt was nearly brushing mine.

"Status of the tunnels is unknown, and we aren't going to travel down into them to find out, either." Duncan leapt up into the back of the truck, grabbing bags and looking at what was packed, his forearms flexing with every move.

Widow Herbert nudged me with her elbow, giving me a knowing smile.

"Then how are we getting across? We're on an island," I said.

"We're going to pick up a boat."

"I haven't been on a boat in decades. That sounds wonderful," Widow Herbert said. "Charlie, we're going boating!"

Charlie was jumping up and down, feeding off her excitement. The two of them were surprisingly perfect companions. She was an adrenaline junkie, and he was five and excited over everything. I was beginning to feel like the only adult in the room.

We piled into the trucks. Buddie and Duncan came in the red one with us, and the other guys piled in the yellow. Widow Herbert and I kept Charlie in the center, afraid of what he might see as we went.

This was the farthest I'd traveled from home since Death Day, and I was glad Widow Herbert was chatting and keeping Charlie distracted. I could feel my hands shaking, my composure slipping, as we drove through what was left of the city: the piled-up cars, bodies littering the street, the silence of the place that used to be bustling with energy. Buddie rolled up the windows at one point, putting on the air as the smell of decomposing bodies grew so strong it was hard to breathe. Every time I thought I'd come to terms with what happened, I'd have another reality check like this.

The trucks took a turn down a smaller road and then finally stopped.

"The marina is a couple of blocks from here. We don't want to give them notice of our arrival," Buddie said.

I leaned toward the front seat. "*Them*?"

"You'd be surprised how many people are looking for boats. There are people who've taken over the marinas," Duncan said, and then got out of the truck.

He opened up the back door, and I handed Charlie over to him then scrambled down fast enough that he didn't have a chance to touch me. My cheeks had already been burning when Widow Herbert caught me staring at his arms. The last thing I needed was for Duncan to get the wrong impression and think I liked him because I was so awkward.

He pointedly looked at Widow Herbert and Charlie, and then back to me. "If you haven't prepared them, you might want to have that chat now."

"She knows enough, and she's tougher than she looks," I said. At least, I hoped she was up for this. I'd seen friendlier-looking monsters in the worst horror movies. Yet Widow Herbert was one of the toughest people I'd ever met, and that group included current monsters.

Duncan looked at her with a raised brow.

"You do what you need to and I'll be just fine," Widow Herbert said.

He didn't look sold.

"What about Charlie?" he asked.

"What about me?" Charlie asked.

"Nothing. The guys might play dress-up later," I said.

All five guys gave me a matching look of distaste. Someone might've made a puking sound.

"Can we just go and let me handle my family as I see fit?"

Duncan gave me another one of those looks like I was shielding the kid too much, but then started walking. Everyone else followed suit.

We started making our way through a network of alleys that they must've plotted out ahead of time.

We could see a sliver of the marina from where we stopped.

"We're going to try to lure them out with a loud noise," Duncan said, and then turned to me. "You three are going to hang back here until we come for you."

"Why would you use a loud noise? They'll come running

out already on the defensive." It was the stupidest plan I'd ever heard. Was that what happened when you could shift into a monster? Finesse went out the window? Your entire arsenal was a battering-ram approach?

"Do you have a better suggestion?" he asked.

I was here because I'd forced an invitation, but damned if I'd be viewed as dead weight. Had I been getting by on my own, while also taking care of a kid and paying Frank's tax? Yes, but barely. Was life better with them around? Without a doubt. I wanted them to want me there.

"I'll lure them out," I said.

The guys, except for Duncan, looked at me as if they approved. Widow Herbert even looked as if she were mulling over the value of sending me in.

Buddie nodded. "I think it's a good—"

"Horrible idea," Duncan said.

"Why? It'll flush them out," I said.

"I think it's a marvelous idea," Widow Herbert said. "They won't view you as a threat."

"I think you let her go," Trevor said. "I've seen her. She's scrappy. She can handle it." He gave me a thumbs-up.

Everyone was staring at Duncan, as if they couldn't quite fathom what the problem was. I certainly didn't know.

"It does make the most sense," Rastin added softly.

"You're going to be close. What's the worst that could happen?" I asked.

Duncan's jaw flexed, and then he moved his head, cracking his neck.

"Fine," he said. "Get to that first boat on the left. There's no lower deck—less chance of a surprise. Once you get onboard, act like you're checking it out. If there are people watching, it'll flush out at least one."

I nodded, though I couldn't make out what boat he was talking about. How good were his eyes? I was afraid to point out that I wasn't sure of the target because he'd barely agreed to the plan as it was.

Duncan looked around the area. "Rastin, Trevor, Birdie, take the east side, over by that building there. Buddie, you stay with me and we'll move up over there."

"What about them?" I looked at Charlie and Widow Herbert.

"They'll stay here." Duncan dug out the keys to the monster truck and grabbed one of his guns to hand to Widow Herbert. "In case things go bad. For some reason, I think you'll manage."

"Me? Oh, I'll get by somehow or another," she said with a knowing smirk.

"Piper." Charlie reached out, grabbing on to my leg.

"Duncan is being silly. It's fine. Everyone is going to make it." I lifted him to my hip and pointed to the boats in the distance. "See those boats? I'm going to go pick out our boat, and then we're going on an adventure."

"Promise?"

"Yes." I gave him a hug, determined to keep my word. "Now you have to stay and take care of Widow Herbert while I go, okay?"

He nodded, walking over to her and grabbing her hand. He put his chin up, taking his job seriously.

I wasn't sure how I'd gone from the sister who barely knew him to whatever this was. I hadn't wanted this responsibility, and yet I couldn't comprehend not having him now. The idea of not getting back to him ripped me apart inside. I was going to figure out how to give him a good life, no matter what I had to do. I'd crawl through the muck so that he could climb to the top of the mountains. I didn't care. Whatever had to be done, I'd do it.

Buddie handed me a gun from his bag. "You know how to use this?"

It didn't look too hard, as long as I didn't have to actually hit something. "You pull this back, aim, and shoot?"

"That's about it," he said. "Tuck it in your jacket."

"Don't go off script. You go to *that* boat, and *stay* there. If someone comes at you, you run back toward us the same way. Don't run deeper into the marina," Duncan said.

"I got it." I walked out of the alley and headed in the direction of the marina gates. I walked slowly, but confidently, as if I weren't doing anything wrong.

The place seemed empty, but there was a feeling of eyes on me. There was at least one person paying attention. These last couple weeks I'd started to develop a sixth sense where I could feel when I was being watched. I kept walking, heading toward the boat Duncan had picked and trying to not give away any hint I was anything but an idiot out for a stroll.

I caught a movement out of the corner of my eye but ignored it, continuing to walk toward my target.

"Hey," a male voice called.

There was a man walking in my direction. He didn't look much older than me, and he certainly didn't seem very intimidating. He reminded me a bit of Pete, the pizza guy. I had to fight back a pang of something soft and mushy that had no place in my life right now.

"I just wanted to look around," I said, shrugging.

"My people run this place. You can't stroll around here." He kept approaching, but slower now, as if he thought I'd run.

"But I need a boat, and you have all these sitting around and not being used." I sounded so stupid that I was afraid no one would believe I'd survived a month of the apocalypse being this idiotic.

He took a couple more steps toward me, and I took another few back. I caught sight of a few more shadowy movements on a large boat a few slips away.

Duncan had said go to the one boat. If I had to run, leave the way I came in. But if I ignored that, and I left in the other direction, it would lure out the people watching me on that other boat.

"Are you hungry?" the guy said.

Yeah, this definitely wasn't Pete. The look in his eyes wasn't anything like the nice guy I'd known. Pete had been a guppy. This guy was a shark, or a barracuda at the least.

"No, I'm good."

He was trying to narrow the gap between us. The guys were going to charge over here any second, and the other threats were still lurking on the bigger boat. If I ran in that direction, they might run out and try to intercept me. Duncan's instructions were good, but he hadn't had this knowledge.

I started running down the pier, away from the shark and in the opposite direction of the way I'd come. I saw people scurrying up on the deck of the big boat and then jumping off in my direction as I ran. I managed to get past them, but just barely, and keep running.

There was shouting behind me, and I was running out of places to go. Taking a sharp left, I followed the walk so I didn't have to jump into the water.

I ran until I hit a brick wall whose arms went around me like a vise.

"Do you not understand instructions?" Duncan said.

There was some screaming behind me—not that he seemed concerned.

115

I pushed out of his arms. "I made a judgment call," I said, trying to get my wind back.

I turned around, seeing several men on the ground and another few running for their lives out of the marina. "It looks like it was a good one."

"Hey, Duncan, what about that beauty?" Buddie yelled, pointing to the nicest yacht in the marina.

"We'll discuss this later," Duncan said, and then walked toward Buddie.

Yeah, that was what he thought.

"Do we have enough gas for that one?" he yelled.

"It's already got some canisters on deck. I'll see what we've got."

"If we can do it, fine." He looked at me and pointed, as if I wasn't ready to skip my way over to that yacht.

Yes, this boat was *definitely* a yacht. As a rule, the apocalypse had sucked up until this point. But this part might actually be a little fun.

Fifteen minutes later, Duncan, Birdie, and Rastin were up at the helm as they drove us out of the marina toward open water. "Do we get to sleep on this thing?" Charlie asked, bouncing up and down like someone had given him new batteries.

Buddie was heading below deck.

"Can I come?" Charlie tagged along with him, not waiting for an answer.

"Listen to whatever he says," I yelled after him.

"We got fishing gear!" Trevor yelled up from the deck below.

Widow Herbert settled onto a blue-and-white-striped deck lounge like she'd been doing this her entire life.

I joined her, lying there and feeling all the adrenaline drain out of me. The yacht was the most luxurious thing I'd ever been on.

"I think we've got a few minutes of peace again. Better enjoy it," she said.

"I'm going to try."

I closed my eyes, feeling the breeze wash over me.

Chapter Sixteen

I WOKE up on the deck to the sun setting over the ocean. I'd come up here for a few minutes after dinner and passed out. It was like my body was trying to catch up on all the missed sleep in the last two days.

Duncan was watching me from where he leaned on the rail, not far away. The two of us were the only ones left on deck.

Where was Charlie? What if he was playing in the engine room or hanging off the back edge? I moved to get up.

"Widow Herbert and Charlie went below early to crash," Duncan said, as if he'd read the cause of the anxiety creasing my brow.

"Thanks." I settled back down, pulling up the blanket someone had draped over me.

Everything was quiet, too peaceful for the world we lived in now. I leaned back, trying to pretend everything hadn't changed for a few minutes. It had become my favorite pastime lately, plucking out little moments in time where I could pretend that the world hadn't died, that I wasn't responsible for another life, that my choices wouldn't possibly doom him as well.

"How long will we be on board?" I said. We'd only just gotten on this boat, and I already dreaded leaving this little bubble, not knowing what was going to come. I didn't want to land. I wanted to float around like this forever.

"A few days, depending on the current."

As he walked along the deck, I noticed a strange-looking phone in his hand.

"What is that?"

"Satellite phone," he said as he dialed and put it to his ear. "We're on our way," he said to whomever he called. He leaned on the railing again. "I'm guessing about a week."

He glanced my way. "Can't be helped."

That certainly couldn't have been more obvious. I tried to focus on the water, the beauty of the night, but couldn't seem to wipe him out of my awareness.

His jaw flexed. "I'll explain when we get there." He ended the call and tossed the phone down on the nearest cushion as if he wished he could've tossed it in the ocean.

I looked at the phone, trying to remember the last call I'd made. "Will that call anywhere?"

"Anyone with a satellite phone."

"So you could call Spain, or Australia, or China, even?"

"Yes, and the situation is the same everywhere or we'd be boating there instead, trust me."

That was what I'd heard, but it was hard not to hope it wasn't true. I thought of people I'd want to call. I had a few friends out on the West Coast, but if they were alive, none of them would have a satellite phone. I wasn't sure I wanted to call and get a head count anyway. It was nicer pretending they were all still alive and that maybe I'd see them again one day.

"Does anyone know what happened? Why everyone died?" He'd obviously spoken to more people than I had.

"No one knows, but it happened at the exact same time everywhere."

I moved the blanket to the side, getting ready to go inside.

"Before you leave, we need to talk."

I sighed and didn't bother trying to hide it. "I'm too tired right now, and I need to check on Charlie."

I'd thought I was going to dodge this conversation. I'd handled the situation the best way and it had worked perfectly, but he still had an issue. I should've left before he got off the phone.

I got up and went to move past him to the door inside, but he was in my way. The closer I was to him, the larger he felt. His scent filled the air all around me, and there was something wild about it, like I was breathing in the rainforest.

"I told you to go on the one boat and stay there."

"I had to make a spur-of-the-moment call, and it turned out better. So…" I threw my hands up, shrugging.

He shook his head, not budging. "That's not how this works. You're part of my pack at the moment. It's like being in the army. I give you an order, and you follow it. You don't deviate."

He was leaning over me in a clear intimidation tactic, speaking to me like all he had to do was make me fully aware of his rules and I'd obey. I wasn't sure if I should disillusion him now or let him be surprised along the way when it didn't work so well.

"My way was better." I moved to squeeze past him, my back along the rail. All it did was give him the chance to cage me against the side of the boat.

"What would've happened if they got to you before I did?" he said.

"But they didn't." I eyed up my exit strategy and was having a hard time finding one. So much for disillusion. I should've opted for surprise.

"If they'd gotten hold of you, they could've used you to hold us off, and there wouldn't have been anything we could've done. You'd be gone."

He was staring at me as if he'd have cared, as if this would've really been a problem for him. As if my dying would've bothered him for even a split second.

"Just a reminder, I'm fairly certain you don't like me. You wouldn't have let me come if I hadn't saved Buddie. If they'd gotten me, you probably would've been cracking open the champagne right now and been three humans lighter, so I'm a little perplexed on what the issue is?"

Heat flared in his eyes as they shifted to my mouth. "You're tough for a human."

I was pretty sure that was his idea of a compliment, and it threw me off guard. It made me break eye contact and look past him. "I'm what I have to be."

"Lots of people crack under conditions like this," he said, his eyes burning into me, and it was as if the air between us was changing, heating, almost sizzling.

"Well, I've got a kid to look out for." I dropped my gaze to the floor, never having been good with compliments, and it seemed even worse when delivered by him.

"And your father didn't?" His voice grew deeper, almost gravelly, feeling like a purr to my senses.

"I'm doing what I have to. That doesn't warrant any special medals."

He wasn't moving. What was most disturbing about this

situation was that I wasn't trying to make him. My breathing was growing raspy, and I had to fight to keep my spine from curving, eating up the tiny distance it would take to make our bodies flush. He was a force of gravity, pulling me closer even when I knew I shouldn't.

"Hey, Duncan, you taking…" Birdie's voice trailed off. "Sorry. Didn't mean to interrupt."

"You didn't," Duncan said, putting space between us. "We were just talking, but we're done."

I waited for him to leave and then nearly ran to my bedroom downstairs.

Chapter Seventeen

I WAS LEANING on the railing of the front of the boat as we crept our way down the Potomac River in Virginia.

Buddie had come out on deck a few minutes ago with a set of binoculars.

"What are you looking for?" I asked.

"Lack of life. We don't want to pull up and have a marina situation like where we left. With all these private docks, it should be doable," he said.

Duncan walked out. I'd been trying to avoid him for the last couple of days, which was hard on a boat. I'd done my best to at least not be alone with him. It seemed as if we'd had a common goal in that.

"Don't look for something too large," Widow Herbert said as she joined us with Charlie. "Survivors are more likely to find a bigger house to congregate at. Look for a little place. That way, if there are people there, they won't feel as secure causing a problem."

Buddie and Duncan looked at each other then back over their shoulders at her.

"You have army training or something?" Duncan asked.

"Psychologist for forty years."

Duncan nodded, and I thought I caught Buddie giving Duncan an *I told you so* glance, as if he'd gone to bat for Widow Herbert in private.

I squinted, spying a small dock in disrepair a bit farther down. "What about that little one with the missing boards?"

Buddie and Widow Herbert nodded.

"That's our target," Duncan said. He motioned up to the helm, where Trevor was steering the boat, and pointed to the dock up ahead.

"Time to pack up," Buddie said.

I went below deck with Widow Herbert and started repacking the few things I'd scattered around the cabin while we were on the water. I swung the loaded pack up onto my shoulders but didn't move. "Maybe we should let them go and stay on this boat."

She gave me one of those smiles that was bittersweet. "You know that's not a good idea."

"Isn't it?" How hard could driving a boat be? Life on here was so peaceful. No one could get to us.

"One, you'll need more insulin for Charlie. You have to find a reliable source. Then there's the problem of running out of gas, and what about when the mechanics on the boat start to break? We get stuck on the water, there is no coast guard to tug us in. As nice as it is, this isn't sustainable."

She was right. I *knew* she was right. I'd thought of all of those things, but on this boat, I could pretend that life hadn't ended. Once I went out on that dock, reality was all there again, a sucking void of desperation, pulling me down like quicksand.

"It'll get better," Widow Herbert said, putting a hand on my shoulder.

"I wish I could be as calm as you." She was in her nineties and woke up with a smile every day. I was twenty and freaking out daily. Maybe I was just a lousy survivor. How had I not died when so many other people who were tougher than me had?

"It's different for me. This life owes me nothing. In some ways, it's easier to live when you've already accepted your death. Fear comes from having something to lose, whatever that may be. Most of the people I loved died already. When the time comes, I know I'll see them again, and it brings me peace." She packed her picture of Walter. "I'll miss you and Charlie, but it's easier knowing you'll have Duncan and the guys."

Putting faith in Duncan and Buddie? No. I tried to smile, not wanting to take that assurance from her, but I wasn't going to rely on anyone. I'd done what I had to with the options available. When a better situation showed itself, I'd grab it with both hands.

I grabbed Widow Herbert's bag and headed upstairs as we were pulling up close to the dock. Buddie leapt over the edge. Trevor followed a second later. They scouted out the area for a few minutes.

"I'm not picking up any recent scents," Buddie said.

Duncan threw over the rope to tie off as I was still digesting that Buddie could smell that well.

Duncan literally tossed us, one by one, to Trevor or Buddie waiting on the dock. Then he jumped off the boat last.

I couldn't believe we were leaving the boat here to rot.

"We'll head inland from here and should be there in a few days," Duncan said.

"We're going to walk the rest of the way?" I asked.

Widow Herbert and Charlie were both in hiking boots, but that didn't mean they'd be able to keep going for miles.

The widow let out a loud sigh. "Okay, I know what everyone is thinking, so we might as well lay it out on the table." She lifted her cane and pointed it at Rastin. "We all know he's going to be dead weight. It's all right, though, because I'll just hit him with my cane if he starts slowing us down."

Rastin laughed as Buddie walked over and motioned to his back. "Get on," he said.

"If you insist," she said. Trevor took her bag while Widow Herbert climbed onto Buddie's back.

"Charlie," Duncan called, and then held out his hand.

Charlie's little face was lit up at having Duncan's attention. He came running past me and grabbed Duncan's outstretched hand. In one smooth motion, he swung my brother up and onto his shoulders. It looked like a move they'd done a thousand times. When had this happened? When had they gotten so chummy? Of all the people Charlie could take to, he had to like Duncan the most? *Him*?

"When you would fall asleep early, Charlie would sneak up on deck and hang out with Duncan," Widow Herbert said, leaning toward me. "Don't worry. Duncan seems to be good with kids."

Rastin raised a brow in my direction, and Duncan swung to look our way, as if he had some interest in my decision.

"I'm fine walking," I said.

"Thank fucking God," Rastin replied.

"Let's head out," Duncan said.

. . .

I soon lived to regret those words. Even with their carrying extra people on their back, I was barely keeping up with the guys.

We were five hours in, having only stopped for a few minutes here and there because someone needed to readjust a boot, or there was a call to nature. I'd take those opportunities to guzzle down water before they moved again. The only glimmer of hope I had of staying off Rastin's back was the sun setting. They couldn't possibly want to keep going in the dark, could they?

"Let's stop here for the night," Duncan called out fifteen minutes later.

I dropped my bags right where I stood, not taking a step farther. My feet weren't capable of it. It felt like I had two gigantic blisters attached to my legs.

"I'll go catch dinner," Duncan said.

He walked right into the tree line, and then I watched as he yanked his shirt over his head. His hands moved to his waist, and I turned before I saw any more. He was catching us dinner, but he didn't have any hunting equipment with him, and now he was stripping.

Charlie tugged on my shirt. "Can I go with Duncan?" He pointed toward where Duncan had disappeared.

"I think he's already gone, but maybe next time." Why did I even say that? I'd never let him go. The kid would be scarred for life. He was too little to realize that his new friend turned into something worse than the boogieman he thought was under his bed.

I knelt on the ground and looked at my supplies, not quite sure what to do with myself. I'd never camped. I hadn't even glamped or slept in a tent in a friend's yard. Bugs freaked me out. Critters made me scream. The closest I'd ever gotten to earthy was some organic oil and diffuser reeds I'd bought in a nice-smelling shop in the mall.

I looked around the forest and couldn't help but wonder why we weren't staying in one of those houses we'd passed along the way. There were plenty of empty ones and we had to sleep here? On the dirt? With creepy-crawly things?

"Are you sure you guys don't want to go a little bit farther, maybe to the next development we hit?" It would be worth the additional torture on my feet to have a normal roof. My feet could completely fall off and I'd crawl there if I had the option.

"No. We won't see someone coming at us, and it messes with the smells," Buddie said.

Apparently I was traveling with bloodhounds.

I glanced around the darkening forest. I wasn't running this show—I'd barely gotten an invite—so I needed to go with the flow. But still, this flow was feeling a little like what ran through the sewage pipes.

"What about bears and other—"

"Monsters?" Rastin laughed. "Yeah, that's not a problem. They won't come near us. We're the top of the food chain."

The world really had gone to hell. "Top of the food chain" used to be penthouse suites. Now it was the best patch of dirt.

"Charlie, look around and gather up little twigs and branches," Buddie said.

"I'll clear out an area for the fire," Widow Herbert said, and then looked at me. "You should probably start on our tent."

"I don't know how to make a tent," I said, trying to keep my voice low enough that everyone didn't hear me. I wasn't sure that was possible.

"Neither do I, and you can't teach an old gal new tricks, so go hop on that." She laughed softly and then moved to her self-designated job.

Dammit. One of us was going to have to get that thing up.

I grabbed the tiny package that had been attached to my pack. This little thing was going to become a tent? I'd seen dollhouses bigger than this. How were the three of us going to sleep in this thing?

I glanced around at the rest of the group, looking for someone to follow. No one else was pulling out a tent. They were all spreading out sleeping bags.

I pulled the contents out, and little poles hit the ground with a clank. There were more parts than I anticipated, but the bag had directions in it. Too bad it was getting dark.

Birdie, who didn't talk much, kept glancing my way and shaking his head.

"What? Is my reading upsetting you? Too uppity for your sensibilities?"

He walked over, threaded some poles through the material sleeves, and then attached them.

"You do the other part of the cross and then stake the corners," he said, not waiting for me to help as he told me what to do. He had my tent up in less than five minutes.

"Thanks," I said.

He nodded.

Duncan came back a few minutes later. I tried to ignore whatever it was that ended up on the fire. I wasn't a vegetarian, but I also wasn't used to being this close to the murder of my food. It was utterly hypocritical, a moral shortcoming that I'd pile with the rest of my issues to be dealt with when this hell was over. So yeah, I was probably off the hook in this lifetime.

I could feel Duncan's eyes on me. I could always feel his

eyes on me. Somehow when he was around, I had some sort of laser focus, probably because he was the biggest threat in the area. It was the only thing that made sense, because I refused to be attracted to someone who turned into one of those creatures. That was too crazy even for the apocalypse.

He walked closer to where I'd set up my tent, and then spread his sleeping bag not even five feet from it. There was all this space, and he had to crowd my tent? Wasn't there some kind of camping etiquette? Birdie obviously felt crowded too, because he then slid his bag farther away. Buddie picked up his and moved it farther away as well. A minute later, Rastin was moving his. Was he the only one who didn't have camping etiquette?

My tent was staked into the ground, and I wasn't going to risk messing with Birdie's work. It was easier to pretend I was alone, sorting through my pack. It wasn't difficult because it felt like all the guys seemed to be giving me a buffer since Duncan returned.

Widow Herbert brought over a few plates of food. I thought I was going to have to tie Charlie down in order to get him to eat. He was running around as if this camping stuff was a dream come true. The guys were all playing with him and treating him normally.

I glanced at Widow Herbert and made a point of looking around the camp and then back to her.

She shrugged. She was obviously noticing the weird behavior too. At least I wasn't crazy.

Duncan wasn't eating at all but leaning against a nearby tree. Even though he wasn't looking at me, I still felt like I had all of his attention. Had I done something wrong? Stepped on someone's toes somehow?

"I'm going to wash up," I said, getting to my feet.

Duncan pushed off the tree and followed me.

"I don't need you to come with me," I said.

"I was headed that way myself. Might as well go together."

That was doubtful, but I went back to ignoring him. He was antsy for some reason I couldn't decipher, but that didn't seem to stop it from flowing off him and rattling my cage.

I made it all of five minutes before I asked, "Is there some sort of issue? You stub a toe while you were out hunting or something?"

"No."

That was it. A fast, short, and definitely bent-out-of-shape denial. I went back to ignoring him. I'd have called anyone a liar an hour ago if they told me I'd be itching to get back on the road, blisters or not. Of course, that was before I had realized Duncan was going to be my personal shadow.

I finished refilling our canteens, washed up the best I could with an audience, and headed back to camp. Once there, I went straight into the tent.

The tent might've said it slept three, but it was one and a half at best unless you slept like sardines. Charlie kicked me in the back five times, as if it had a target painted on it. Two hours later and the patch of dirt outside looked like a memory foam mattress. I left the two of them snoring away as I crept out and settled my bag by the fire. I was so exhausted that it didn't matter where I lay down. I was out in minutes.

I woke to soft sounds of talking.

"How could I *not* notice? We all noticed," Birdie whispered. "You don't think…"

"Nah. Sometimes it just hits weird but then never happens again. You know how it is," Rastin said.

"Yeah, but it was intense, you know?" Buddie chimed in.

"That didn't feel like it was an off night. We've all had off nights. The shit he was putting off…"

I knew I hadn't been imagining it. Everyone thought Duncan had been acting nuts.

"Look, whatever it is, it doesn't matter because it can't. We need to just ignore it. It's none of our business," Rastin said.

"Yeah, but that doesn't usually work. It doesn't when it's normal," Trevor said. "He shifted, and it kicked into high gear."

"There's no way that was normal. It was an anomaly probably triggered by all the crazy shit going on," Rastin said.

"Yeah, that is a good point. Nothing is normal, so why would that be?" Buddie said.

"Yeah, so let's not talk about it anymore," Rastin said. "Last thing we need is for him to come back and hear us talking about—"

Buddie cleared his throat. "I don't think we should be discussing this at all."

My eyes were closed, but I couldn't lose the feeling of their attention shifting to me.

"I'm hitting the hay," Rastin said. I heard the rest of them shifting around, and the conversation was definitely over.

Whatever Duncan's issue was, they didn't want me to hear about it. Maybe stress made shifters weird or something. It didn't sound like it was something I had caused anyway, and that was all that mattered to me. It was Duncan's problem.

Chapter Eighteen

WHATEVER DUNCAN'S problem had been last night, he seemed back to himself and all business today. Everyone seemed so normal as we packed up the camp that if I hadn't heard the guys talking, I would've thought I'd imagined the weirdness.

Charlie was swung up onto Duncan's shoulders, and Widow Herbert climbed onto Buddie's back. Rastin didn't offer me a ride, not that I would've accepted.

We'd been walking a couple hours when we stopped at the bank of a river. It was a relief to stop at all for any reason. I'd stopped feeling parts of my feet an hour ago, and instead of being alarmed, I felt relief.

"We'll cross here," Duncan said. "It's unlikely we'll hit a calmer point."

Wait, what?

They wanted to take Charlie, a five-year-old, and Widow Herbert, in her nineties, across this? I was familiar enough with rivers to know that even if it didn't look like full-blown rapids, if I could see the current, it wasn't going to be easy to cross.

"Isn't there a bridge somewhere?" I asked.

"Bridges are the worst possible places to cross. Deathtraps if they're still intact," Buddie said. "We aren't immortal. We can be killed like anything else. Shoot us up with enough bullets and we're dead. Not to mention it's unclear how many bullets you guys could take."

"Closest one is going to take us hours out of our way," Rastin said.

I was still looking for a way out of this while Duncan sized up who should go first. "Buddie, you take Charlie. Rastin, you carry Widow Herbert, and I'll take Piper."

"Wait, you're the strongest, right?" I asked Duncan, not caring if I was stepping on some male egos. I'd stomp on them like they were potato chips if needed to get Charlie across safely.

"Yes," he answered, and no one so much as blinked.

"You take Charlie."

He looked like he was mulling it over before he said, "He's smaller. It'll be better if—"

"I don't care," I said, ready to die on this hill, or maybe more accurately, drown in this river. "He's the only one here who didn't get a choice in making this trip. He crosses with you. Widow Herbert gets the next strongest. I'll cross on my own."

Duncan took a second, as if working out the weights in his mind. "If you want me to cross with Charlie, that's fine, but you'll never make it across alone. You go with Rastin."

"You want me to cross with Piper?" Rastin asked, as if Duncan hadn't said it less than a second ago.

"Yes. It's fine," Duncan replied, even though his jaw seemed clenched as he spoke.

And *there* it was again. That weird thing going on. Except I couldn't worry about it right now, because I was going to cross rapids on someone's back. Worse than that, I'd be watching someone else carry Charlie across. I wasn't going to have too much time to dwell on it, as Birdie was already heading in, testing the waters, since he wasn't carrying anyone. One by one, we all slowly entered the river behind him.

"Make sure you hold on. I need my arms for balance. I can't keep you glued to my back, too." Rastin might've seemed okay carrying me, but he definitely wasn't enjoying it.

"I think I can manage." I wrapped my arms a little tighter than necessary around his neck.

"As much as I might annoy you, you probably want to make sure I can breathe as we cross." He laughed.

"Fine." I loosened my grip. It was hard to be annoyed at someone who laughed at my attempts to kill them, while carrying me across the rapids.

Even lugging me around, Rastin seemed sure-footed. The water was cold enough to make you gasp for breath.

We'd made it a third of the way across and the water had only hit their thighs when suddenly Birdie was waist deep. He got his bearings back fast enough. Duncan seemed unfazed, and Charlie looked back at me, face lit with excitement and waving a hand.

"Look forward and hold on with both hands," I yelled, wondering when I'd turned into this person. I sounded like a soccer mom or something, and I didn't care. That kid better keep his hands glued to Duncan.

He gave me the *you're no fun* look but did what I asked.

By the time we hit the midpoint, the water was up to our chests. Rastin's footing slipped. In a blink, we were four feet farther downstream and my heart was six inches higher and sitting in my throat. How had he slipped? His body was like solid iron beneath me. If he was struggling, I'd have been dead already.

Duncan watched and waited.

"We're good," Rastin yelled, and Duncan started moving again.

I wanted to close my eyes, but then I'd lose sight of Charlie if he needed me. I didn't breathe until we slowly emerged from the water. I could feel the weary exhaustion in Rastin's frame. I dropped my legs and slid down his back, and kept right on going until I was laid out flat on the ground.

Charlie was jumping around as if he'd gotten off the best amusement park ride ever made. I closed my eyes for a minute, waiting for my heart to go back into place.

"Hey, something's not right over here," Buddie yelled.

My eyes shot open as he laid Widow Herbert on the ground.

I'd been so consumed with Charlie, I hadn't even checked on Widow Herbert. How could I have not thought about her? I pushed myself upright and rushed to her side.

"What's wrong?" I asked, grabbing her hand.

"It's tight," she said, putting a hand to her chest.

Duncan put his fingers to her neck and then his ear to her chest. "She's having a heart attack."

"How? Why? I don't understand. She doesn't have a heart problem." I gripped her hand with both of mine, hating the chill of her skin.

"Might've been the cold, the excitement. It's hard to know. She's older. Anything could've triggered it," Duncan said.

"What do we do?" I looked at Duncan, and then the rest of

them, who were all standing around doing nothing. "What about CPR? We can do CPR." I positioned myself over Widow Herbert's chest, but Duncan pulled me back.

"No," she said, shaking her head.

"You're just going to cause her pain. CPR is good to try to keep enough oxygen to the rest of the body as a stopgap, but it's not going to save her," Duncan said.

"What about your satellite phone? Can't you call someone?"

"Who? There is no one to call. There are no emergency services," he said calmly.

I knew that. Of course I did. But the reality hadn't hit home quite like this before. She was having a heart attack, and if it had been two months ago, there would be an ambulance on its way and doctors waiting at a hospital.

Now, she was having a heart attack and everyone was standing around accepting that she was going to die.

Except for me.

"Hang on. You can make it through this." I grabbed her hand again, deciding she was going to make it by the sheer force of my determination. "Someone get a bag and put it under her feet to help her blood flow."

They all looked at me as if I were the one who needed help right now.

"I need a bag!"

"Piper." Widow Herbert's eyelids were drooping, and I could see the pain in her expression. "It's okay. I'm okay."

I squeezed her hand tighter. "Please stay with me. I don't want to be selfish, but I need you. You *can't* die." Nothing about this was okay. I'd dragged her out here with me, and now she was dying.

"If I could stay for you, I would. But this body is done with me, and they're already waiting." She glanced to her other side and smiled, as if she were looking at people. "You'll be okay. You're so much tougher than you realize. You and Charlie will be fine without me."

"Please, please, please try to stay?" Tears started coursing down my cheeks in rivers, and I didn't care who saw.

"Don't be sad. I'm ready. I've *been* ready. I'm glad I got a last adventure before I go to be with Walter. Wait until I tell him about these last few days. He's going to get such a kick out of it." She looked to the side again, smiling. I saw her other hand lift, and she closed her fingers as if wrapping them around something only she could see.

"Please don't leave me," I said, but she was looking off and I wasn't sure she even heard me anymore. Her eyes went still. Her face went slack.

"Piper," Duncan said.

"Give me a minute." I was bent over Widow Herbert's body. I didn't want to talk to anyone. I wanted to be left alone.

"Piper," he repeated softly.

"Please, leave. Me. Be."

"She's gone?" Charlie asked, and I realized Duncan had been trying to give me a heads-up.

Not only was Widow Herbert dead, but I'd forgotten about Charlie watching her pass. How had I forgotten him? I'd pulled him from his home, dragged him off with monsters on a trip dangerous enough that we'd already lost one person, and now I'd probably traumatized him.

I looked up, wiping the tears from my eyes, preparing to say who knew what, but Duncan knelt beside him.

"She's not gone," he said softly. "She's moved on to a new place. We each get so many years here before we move. She learned what she needed from this world, this body. She fulfilled her purpose and now has other things to do in other places."

"But her body is still here?" Charlie asked, looking at Widow Herbert's still form.

"That's only the skin and tissue she left behind. The part that counts, the part that made you laugh and played with you and told you stories? The important parts? That's what moves on to something new and wonderful."

Charlie leaned close and wrapped his arms around Duncan's neck.

Duncan lifted him up and then nodded to Buddie. "Why don't you take him to go set up camp?"

Buddie took Charlie, and they disappeared into the woods, with the other guys following him.

I found the sharpest, flattest rock I could and began digging with it.

"I'll bury her. Go take care of Charlie," Duncan said. It was only us left in the clearing.

I dropped the rock and nodded. I was having a hard time reconciling the monster that terrified me with the man who had just come up with the perfect words to comfort Charlie.

They were setting up camp not far away. Charlie was walking around, picking up sticks with his head drooping and his feet dragging. Buddie didn't look much better, but he motioned in Charlie's direction, looking lost.

"You okay?" I asked, going over to him. I definitely wasn't, that was for sure.

"Everyone goes away," Charlie said, his lip quivering as his eyes watered.

"No, not everyone." I smoothed my hand over his unruly hair.

"Because you won't leave me, right?"

"I'll never leave you." I pulled him into a hug, again making that promise I knew I shouldn't.

Buddie was kneeling not far from us, poking at the fire he'd just made. He lifted his arms in a monster pose and then shrugged, leaving the decision up to me.

It wasn't like I could go buy him a toy at the moment to help distract him. It was probably better if he started understanding what the guys were now, while I could tell him calmly, rather than be scared out of his mind later, the way I was.

"You know who's really tough and hard to kill?" I said. Was that the right thing to say? Probably not, but this parenting shit was hard under good circumstances.

"Who?"

"Buddie. The other guys too. It takes a lot to get rid of them." If they could hand out parenting grades, I'd definitely be bringing home an F right now. How low I'd sunk.

"It does?" he said, coming around a little.

Buddie looked at me with a brow raised, as if trying to figure out how far we were going to take this.

"It's because there's all different kinds of people in this world. And some people can do extra-special things."

Buddie smiled, holding both thumbs up.

"Like Timmy? He can already skateboard," Charlie said.

"Yes, kind of like that," I agreed, not really wanting to talk about Timmy, since he was dead in a ditch somewhere. "Buddie here can do some extra-crazy stuff." I glanced up at Buddie.

"I can," he agreed.

"Like what?" Charlie asked.

Buddie looked at me, waiting for the call.

How much truth did you give a five-year-old? How was I supposed to know?

"Well, Buddie can make himself look like a monster, and so can the other guys. They aren't really monsters, because they're good, but they can look really scary."

Charlie's eyes doubled in size. "Can I see? Please? Please?"

The kid was nearly vibrating with the urgency to see such a miracle happen. I'd thought he'd be a little hesitant, at least at first.

"He'll look really scary. Are you sure?" I asked.

Buddie's chest was puffing up again, the way it had when Widow Herbert complimented him.

A shudder ran through me at the thought of Widow Herbert. *Don't think of her as dead. Think of her as having moved on to somewhere better, because she has. Or try not to think about her at all right now so I don't fall apart while I'm trying to help Charlie.*

"I'll show you if it's okay with your sister," Buddie said, picking up the slack as I fell silent.

"Show what?" Rastin asked, walking back into the camp.

"The kid wants to see my beast form," Buddie said, nearly gloating.

"If the kid wants to see a monster, I'm the one who should shift," Rastin told him.

"What the hell are you talking about? I should shift," Trevor said, coming over. "I'm the best one here."

"No one is scarier than me," Birdie added.

"Let's have a contest!" Charlie jumped up and down, clapping his hands. "You all do it!"

This was going downhill fast. I didn't want them all

shifting at once because then *I'd* have to see them. Sleep was hard enough.

"Charlie will pick a winner," Rastin said. "I want this to be legit, so you all better shift out of sight so he doesn't know who's who. We don't need any pity winners." He eyed Buddie.

"I don't need a pity vote," Buddie fired back.

I got to my feet. "Maybe we should do this in smaller doses?"

Everyone ignored me as they took off into the woods. Charlie kept jumping up and down.

This had completely spiraled out of my control. The only good thing was that Charlie was no longer thinking of Widow Herbert. Unfortunately, he might be traumatized in a different way in a few minutes. It was becoming clear to me that my parenting skills were severely lacking. My gut on this stuff probably shouldn't be trusted.

I pulled Charlie to me, hugging him for my own sake.

What if he was scared of them for the rest of his life? I tried to hold down the emotional vomit happening within me. I went from utter sadness to terror that I was about to scar this kid for the rest of his life.

Charlie tried to jump around in my arms, laughing and clapping as they walked out.

There they were. Four of them. All monstrous. I wanted to run and scream, and my chest was having a hard time expanding. Charlie was fighting to get out of my embrace, trying to get to them.

I let go, against my better judgment, and he moved closer. His eyes were huge, and his little mouth dropped open in utter awe of them.

"Wow," was all he could say as he reached out and even insisted on touching claws and leathered skin.

One was worse than the next. It didn't help that they started striking poses like it was a weightlifting competition. Some of them were growling as they did, as if it complemented their monsterly physique.

They were really getting into it, too. What the hell were they doing? Tensing up their butts and flexing monster forearms? I tried not to focus on the appendages that were hanging there. At least Charlie was a boy and I wouldn't have to explain that part, although I might have to make sure he didn't get any kind of inadequacy complex.

The more I watched their antics, the more I felt like giggling, and I didn't think that was their intention. The flexing suddenly stopped. There was a little squeak, like the sound of a dog toy. It was a big departure from the growls of moments ago.

"What the hell are you guys doing?" Duncan asked, walking into the clearing.

"It's a contest!" Charlie yelled.

"Oh. Well, now it all makes sense," Duncan said.

"Pick a winner," I said, nudging Charlie.

He walked up and down the line of monsters, who were resuming their poses again, more afraid of losing the contest than being judged by Duncan for looking ridiculous.

Charlie stepped back. "You all win!" he said. "Just like at school," he added.

The monsters stood there, staring, and even I could read the unhappiness they had with that decision in their beady eyes. Poor kid. The days of everyone winning were long gone, if they ever truly existed.

Chapter Nineteen

THE CAMP WAS QUIET, everything calm, Charlie's breathing steady beside me in the tent. But every time I closed my eyes, I saw Widow Herbert dying. I heard myself frantic and screaming, and then seeing Charlie looking at us.

If we hadn't come, she'd probably be alive. She was older, but she might've had a few more years left. How many years had she lost? What if she'd had a decade? People lived till over a hundred every day. She might've been okay with meeting death, but I wasn't good with being the one who'd escorted her to the door.

My chest was tight, and growing worse, like the pressure was building and was going to explode. I'd been holding it in for hours, and I was down to minutes now. I had to get away from everyone before they saw the mess I was about to become.

I crawled out of the tent, slipped on my boots, and tiptoed around the guys who'd formed a circle around the tent. Duncan's spot was empty. This wasn't the first time I'd rolled over and seen him gone, though.

I kept looking back, making sure I didn't lose sight of the fire, but I had to get out of earshot. My body shuddered, and I stopped, leaning against a tree as the day's events finally overwhelmed me. The fear, guilt, and doubt all meshed inside and spilled out of me in a ball of emotional turmoil. I knelt on the ground, my breathing ragged as I tried to retain some amount of control.

Why did the world have to go to shit now? I was too young and stupid to make these choices. I'd gotten Widow Herbert killed, and I still had a five-year-old to take care of.

I was bent over, feeling like I might vomit, when a hand closed over my mouth. Another wrapped around my upper body. I was lifted off my feet. My arms were useless, but I kicked back with everything I had. There were shadows moving on either side of me, so there were at least three people.

I tried to bite the hand covering my mouth, but it was planted too firmly. One good scream and the guys would hear, but I was getting carried farther away.

I didn't stop kicking, but the man carrying me was at least a foot taller and had arms like tree trunks. If I could get out of this grasp, get free to scream for one second…

My captor stumbled on something, and we both fell to the ground. He let go on our way down. I took the brunt of his weight as he fell on top of me, knocking the wind out of me. He wasn't there for long before his body went flying.

There was scrambling, and I looked up in time to see Duncan looming over the man on the ground. There were sounds of running as the other two fled the scene.

"You okay?" he asked, grabbing my hand and pulling me to my feet.

"Give me a minute and I will be." The tremor in my voice said I might be lying.

My would-be abductor was lying on the ground five or so feet away. A large boulder by his head was covered in blood. It looked like the side of his head was caved in. How hard had Duncan thrown him?

"Is he dead?" I asked.

"Yes. Unfortunate landing, for him, anyway," Duncan said. "What were you doing so far from camp?"

"I had to go to the bathroom," I said, grasping at the first excuse that didn't include mental breakdown.

"You don't go this far. It's not safe." It was too dark to see his face, but his voice held an edge of irritation.

"I appreciate your helping me, but that doesn't mean you can tell me what to do. I'm not part of your pack. I make my own choices." I had enough problems without an overbearing monster trying to boss me around. This was not the night to pick a fight with me.

"If you made sound choices, I wouldn't have to tell you the obvious. I don't want to have to worry about your getting grabbed every time I walk away."

He took a step closer to me, and I backed up. My emotions were too raw to have him churning already rough waters.

"I think you're exaggerating a hair, don't you?" I didn't bother hiding my sarcasm.

There was a long pause, and I could feel his eyes boring into me.

"What?" He wasn't speaking, but Duncan wasn't the type to roll over and let me win a fight that easy.

"You don't know, do you? You have no idea." He scoffed, as if he couldn't fathom my ignorance.

"Know what?" I said, making it clear I wasn't going to buy whatever crap he was about to try to feed me.

"Have you not noticed that Death Day took out way more human women than men?"

"That's not…" Wait. Had it? Was it true? I thought back to my apartment building. Of the ten percent of us who hadn't died, only a third of that had been female. Of that third, only about half of them were younger or near childbearing age.

He was right. How had I not realized?

"I see you're starting to comprehend the situation," he said. "After food, water, and the basics to keep living, the next biggest drive is to procreate. A lot of these people have food; there's plenty of shelter. The single biggest lack now are human women of childbearing age.

"That means from here on out, you don't go more than twenty feet away from one of us. Because beyond anything else here, you're going to be what they want. You're the most valuable thing in the camp."

Chapter Twenty

FOR THE FIFTIETH TIME TODAY, I turned to look for Widow Herbert. Had she realized what Duncan had, about more women dying? If she had, why hadn't she mentioned it? There were so many things I wanted to talk to her about, but she was gone. I'd barely known her, and yet her death felt like a gaping hole. I almost never thought of my father, but the loss she left was a harsh void that wouldn't be filled for a long while. Some people were like that; they punched above their weight class in life.

My chest tightened, my eyes began to burn, and I took a few deep breaths. Duncan glanced over his shoulder, as if he'd caught the irregular breathing. His hearing was getting quite annoying when it wasn't being useful. I let my eyes pass over him to settle on the horizon, not acknowledging the attention.

I had to stop thinking of Widow Herbert, or at least wait until I was alone. She'd been okay with passing, and I had to keep reminding myself of that. She'd gone on to something much nicer than where I was probably headed and would be for the foreseeable future. Hell, life would be hard for centuries to come at this rate.

Not to mention how hard it was to get there. How steep was this incline going to get? Duncan slowed to a stop, and everyone else followed suit. I took the opportunity to narrow the gap that had begun to grow. When they didn't continue to walk, I grabbed my canteen and chugged some water. I'd been so busy trying to keep up that I hadn't wanted to waste the seconds it would take to get a drink.

"Buddie, take Charlie," Duncan said, handing my brother over. "I'll get Piper."

"Get me?" I took a step back, and then another.

He turned, giving me his back. "Hop on."

"What?" I stared at him.

"Get on my back. I'll carry you the rest of the way," he said.

"I'm an adult. I can walk."

"What he's not saying is you're slowing us down." Rastin glared at me. "We won't make it there by midnight if we have to keep moving at your pace."

"I'll walk faster," I said.

"Scrappy but stubborn as hell." Trevor rolled his eyes.

"Back or shoulder, those are your only two choices," Duncan said.

"It's fun getting a ride," Charlie called from nearby, trying to console me.

My getting a ride only further cemented what they thought of me: weak, useless human.

Buddie moved closer. "We want to get there tonight," he whispered, trying to soften the message. He leaned in slightly closer, and in a voice I could barely hear, he said, "The incline is going to get worse. You're *not* going to make it."

Worse than what we were already climbing? "How bad?"

"Nearly vertical in places."

Shit.

I looked over at Duncan. "Back."

He turned around. I jumped up, using the last strength I had in my legs to do it.

He grabbed a thigh in each hand, as if he knew I might not manage to stay on if left to my own devices. I would at this point, but I hated that he knew it.

As soon as we started moving again, I realized how much I'd slowed them down. Even with me on Duncan's back, he was nearly jogging most of the way instead of the slow, steady walk we'd been doing before.

We went on like this for hours until Duncan stopped walking, letting go of my legs and letting me slip to the ground. The sun was nearly setting.

"Wait, I get to walk?" I asked, sounding snippy for someone who'd caught a ride for hours. I couldn't seem to stop myself, though, because it felt like Duncan had won this last battle.

"We're almost there. It's better if you walk in," he said, then grinned, as if he knew exactly why I was irritated.

"*There* there? There, as in the place we're going to stay?"

"Yes. Stay near Buddie," he said, and then walked as if putting distance between us.

Did he want me to blend in with the pack? That was fine by me.

"Watch what you say. If you can see someone, there's a good chance that they can hear you," Buddie said, walking beside me, Charlie still on his back.

"I thought we were going to join your people? This doesn't

sound like you trust them." I already had my own apprehensions, and they were growing thicker by the minute.

"They're our people, so to speak, but they aren't *our* pack. They run things a little differently. With the current situation, we've all made the decision to condense. Safety in numbers, you know?"

What were they concerned about? They were the scariest thing around, weren't they? Suddenly I wasn't so sure. Again I wished Widow Herbert was here to bounce ideas off or to tell me it would work out.

"What's the place like?" I asked.

"I've never been there, but it's a historic site they took over after Death Day," Buddie said.

"You mean like Colonial Williamsburg or something?"

"Yes, but more rustic, and a lot more out of the way. Still, it's got the rudimentary structures of everything you need to run a community when there's no longer a modern grid," Buddie said.

We kept walking, and a brick visitors' building popped into view. He wasn't kidding. This was a legitimate historical site. There was a ticket window and everything. My mother had used to love places like this and taken me to any we'd ever been close to.

We walked through turnstiles, and I gazed down the street lined with old log homes and buildings. A lot of them had smoke coming out of the chimneys because they probably all had wood stoves or fireplaces. There were hanging signs for a blacksmith, a weaver, and a printer. There were barns and chicken coops. There was a building that looked like a schoolhouse, and even horses grazing over in the field. Farther out, I spotted some cows and sheep. I hadn't met these people yet, but they'd already gone up a notch in my estimation just for creativity. If the world was regressing, what better place to pick? It was like stepping back in time.

There was no lack of people running around, either, and some were heading our way.

A sandy-haired woman with the brightest blue eyes I'd ever seen walked over. She wasn't classically beautiful, but she had a startling sexuality about her that nearly knocked you to your knees.

"Groza," Duncan greeted her.

"It's great to see you. I'm glad you all made it out," she said, pushing her insanely thick blond hair out of her face. She looked around, greeting the other guys as well. It was obvious they all knew each other.

Her gaze landed on me, and then Charlie, and then there was a slight glance back to Buddie, as if she were trying to peg if there was an attachment there.

"You might want to keep your guests close," she said to Duncan. "I'm not sure how well my people will take to them."

"I'd assumed you'd be able to handle that situation," he said. There was an edge that came just shy of outright insult.

"I'll put the word out, but I don't micromanage my people."

If I'd doubted their reasons for not wanting to bring me, I no longer did. This woman wouldn't give a shit if I got drop-kicked into the nearest ravine. I wouldn't be shocked if she actually encouraged her people to give me a kick or two on my way down.

Hopefully this hadn't been the wrong choice. If it wasn't for Charlie, I wouldn't care what they did. Although if it wasn't for Charlie, I probably would be testing out the waters on my own.

"I don't want to step on toes, but I will," Duncan said.

"There are other ways to fix that, and you know it," she replied.

They were in a stare-off, seeming to have reached some sort of stalemate.

"Come. Let me show you your lodgings," she said, breaking the silence first.

I didn't know enough shifters to gauge if that meant Duncan or Groza had won, or if it had been called a draw. Either way, we started walking down the small lane. People were waving and nodding here and there. The guys broke off to exchange longer hellos.

When Buddie slowed down for a moment, I stayed beside him, not wanting to be far from Charlie.

The guy he was talking to gave me a curious glance but seemed leery of speaking to me. I barely paid attention to their conversation, taking in all that was around instead, until the guy asked Buddie, "How bad were your losses?"

"About half. What about you?" Buddie said.

"Same."

Half? They'd only lost half? It was still a blow, but compared to ninety percent, it seemed like a gift.

"We'll catch up soon," Buddie said, before heading back to the group.

I was debating asking him about it when I spotted an older woman watching us as we walked. A lot of people were watching us, especially me and Charlie, but she was by herself, all in black, and there was something just...*different* about her.

"That would be Jaysa," Buddie said, noticing my attention. "She's the guide of this region."

"Guide? What is that, exactly?" The only place she looked like she'd guide you was into hell.

"It's hard to explain exactly. They're all a little different, and there aren't many, but she senses when things are off and offers suggestions to steer things back on track. She was the one who thought the packs should merge."

"Do you mean magic woo-woo stuff?"

Groza turned her head slightly. I could see her profile and the scowl forming. Great, I'd already forgotten about the hearing issue. This woman already hated me, and that hadn't helped.

"Something like that," Buddie said, shooting me a look.

It was a little late for a warning. I didn't ask anything else, afraid of what might slip out and get me in more trouble.

We kept walking until we were on the edges of the development and she pointed to two small houses. One had a sign for "The Bunny Cottage," and the other said "Doc's Place."

"Doc's has three bedrooms and Bunny has two. You're free to spread out into one of the other buildings as well if you need." Groza glanced at me again.

If we were so welcome, why hadn't she offered another building?

"This will be fine," Duncan said.

It was what I would've said too.

"There are some basics inside. We also have a roast most nights if you want to swing by. I'll leave you to get settled in." She nodded to the rest of the group, dragging her gaze over me and Charlie a little longer than I liked.

"Come by and have a talk once you're settled," she said to Duncan.

He nodded as if she were reminding him he had to go take out the trash or something.

"You guys take Doc's place," he said. "I'll take the Bunny cottage with Pip and Charlie."

Huh? He was staying with me? I mean, I wasn't expecting

a place all to myself, but why couldn't I have gotten Buddie as a roommate? Anyone but Duncan. I couldn't be in the same field without feeling on edge with him. And what was the deal with "Pip"? When had he decided we were close enough he could chop my name in half? It wasn't that no one ever called me Pip, or that I cared before. But why did he think *he* could?

No one said a word as the guys went into Doc's and Duncan went into Bunny's. Charlie ran in after him, forcing my hand.

I either stood out here alone, like an idiot, or I went in and accepted my fate at Bunny's. *Dammit.*

It was charming, I had to give it that. There were wide-planked wooden floors and that smell of a place heated with wood for years. There were only a few rooms on the first floor, a living room, kitchen, and a small bedroom in the back. A narrow, steep set of stairs led to a single room above with two small beds topped with plaid coverlets. A window was centered between the beds, and a wood table was under the opening with an oil lamp on it.

This entire settlement looked like the set of *Little House on the Prairie*, including this cottage. All I could think of was my mother talking about how she wished she could live in one of those sites we'd toured. I had a feeling it wasn't going to be as fun now that there wasn't electricity. But there was still something so earthy and comforting that I wanted to curl up on the bed and take a nap now.

"You should take the second level," Duncan said as I came back downstairs.

That was all Charlie needed to hear before he ran upstairs to settle in.

"How long do you think we'll be here for?" For the time

being, I'd hitched my wagon to this horse, so I was better off being prepared.

"There are some arrangements in place that have to be worked out," he said, not appearing to be any happier about being here than I was.

"Do you think it's going to be...*good* here?" I wasn't exactly on comfy enough terms to ask Duncan if his unfriendly connections were going to try to murder me in my sleep. Considering he'd told me to take upstairs, he might've already been thinking it himself.

"It's not going to be ideal, so I wouldn't be lax until we get things settled."

"Piper! There's a cool old train up here. Can I play with it?" Charlie yelled from above.

I pointed to the stairs. "I'm going to go get him settled."

Chapter Twenty-One

I HAD GONE to the room with Charlie yesterday intending to help him get settled. Putting my head down while he was playing with the train had been a mistake. Now the morning light was waking me up. Again? It was the boat all over. How long had I slept?

Charlie wasn't in the other bed, and I went from barely awake to a five-alarm fire.

"Charlie!" I sprang from the bed and ran toward the stairs.

"I'm here, Piper," he yelled.

"We're eating breakfast," Duncan called from the kitchen area.

I rested a hand on the railing as I spotted Charlie smiling over at me as if everything was right in the world.

Duncan stood in front of a wood stove, flipping pancakes with only a pair of low-hanging sweats on. It was a bit warm in here with the stove going, so I couldn't quite fault him. Still, how was I supposed to live with someone who looked like that and didn't seem to care if he was half-dressed?

"Charlie, you're supposed to wake me when you get up," I

said, ruffling my brother's hair and trying to look anywhere but at Duncan's chiseled abs.

"Duncan told me it was okay to let you sleep because you were so tired."

Oh. Duncan told him. I was starting to resent Duncan's pedestal, and there definitely seemed to be a very tall one involved here. If it were up to Charlie, it would be diamond encrusted, too.

"Are you mad?" Charlie asked, looking confused.

"Of course not." Everything was fine as long as I could keep my eyes off Duncan's body. I couldn't afford hormones, considering the current situation.

Charlie smiled and then stabbed a huge piece of pancake into his mouth. How much had he eaten? That stuff was like eating cake.

I turned to the all-perfect, all-knowing Duncan. "If you're going to feed him, he needs—"

"I already gave it to him." Duncan nodded to the small bottle sitting on the table.

Charlie smiled, as if I'd been silly for doubting Duncan, of all people. Well, I had.

I picked up the vial. "Are you sure you did it—"

"I've been traveling with you for days. I've watched." He gave me one of those *I'm not an idiot* smiles.

I settled at the table, not smiling. The verdict was still out, as far as I was concerned.

"Hungry?" Duncan asked.

I hesitated even though my stomach felt like it was going to self-cannibalize. He was taking over *everything*.

Duncan handed me a plate of pancakes before I could say no. He'd already made them. It would be ridiculous to refuse and then try to sneak a couple bites later. This was not going to become a habit. I'd make sure I got up early with Charlie tomorrow. I couldn't let him get used to this either.

As it was, Charlie and Duncan looked like they'd been hanging out together like this for years, and the whole picture put me on edge. What would happen when Charlie and I went our separate ways from the guys? It would happen eventually. We weren't shifters. We couldn't live in their pack like this forever. Once I figured out a reliable source for insulin, I'd find a place we could go. In the meantime, I had to try to make life as normal for Charlie as possible.

"I thought I saw some kids coming out of a schoolhouse yesterday," I said. Would it be crazy to enter him into a school with nothing but shifter kids? Would it be good for him or better if he didn't mingle at all? Would he be treated as just another kid, or picked on and alienated? But he'd have no friends here if we didn't try, no one to play with. He'd be isolated. None of that might matter because they might not let him attend anyway.

"I have to go to school?" Charlie said, scrunching his face up.

"I'm not sure. I don't know how long we'll be here, but it's a thought." What I was most unsure of was whether they'd let him.

"I'll check into that if you want," Duncan said. He knew this pack better than me.

"I'd appreciate it," I said, making the mistake of looking in his direction again.

He was leaning against the counter, eating pancakes. Even when he was doing nothing, his muscles flexed. It was probably because of those monster genetics. I was lusting after a monster's body.

I pulled my gaze off his abdomen, only to get caught

looking at his pecs for a minute, and then his arms after that. I finally dragged my eyes off his body to see him grinning. He might've been eating, but he hadn't been oblivious to my perusal.

Charlie leaned closer. "Why is your face red?"

"It's hot in here." His question made my face hotter.

He tilted his head, as if gauging the temperature. It must've passed his test, because he let it drop.

"I'm not going to school today, though, right?" Charlie asked. "Duncan told me he'd teach me how to fish today."

I tried to smile and nod. "Charlie, eat your breakfast while I show Duncan something outside."

"But I don't have to go to school today, right?" he pressed.

"No. You're fine," I said. I took a step toward the door and glanced back at Duncan, giving him a look that said he better follow me.

"What is this? What are you doing?" I asked as soon as he stepped outside. "He *likes* you." I said it like it was a cardinal sin.

"I'm likable," he said, then smirked.

"No you're not." Did this man have no self-awareness? He barely spoke, and when he did, it was to boss people around. That was the antithesis of likable.

"You sure?" Now he was grinning like he knew a secret.

"I admired your body. That doesn't mean diddly squat, so get over yourself. And stop smiling so much. What is wrong with you? Why are you acting so weird? And what's with these fishing plans?" It was almost like he was flirting, except Duncan didn't flirt. He grumped and bossed. I leaned against the porch railing, crossing my arms.

He stopped grinning. The bossy, serious Duncan was back. At least I was on familiar footing again.

"Have you ever heard the saying 'teach a man to fish, you feed him for life'?" he asked. He walked closer, putting his hand on the post and leaning a little too close for my comfort. "He needs to learn how to survive. To be honest, it wouldn't hurt for you to know how to fish, either."

When he put it like that, there was no disagreement. He was right. If Charlie was going to survive this world, he needed more skills than I had to teach him.

"Okay. I guess he goes fishing."

"You coming along?" Duncan asked, still leaning in a little too close.

Even if I hadn't decided on another plan for the day, I wasn't going anywhere with Duncan right now. No, the only thing we needed was space in between us.

"I'll go with you next time. I've got something else to do." I was definitely *not* going with him next time. I'd learn from Charlie.

He narrowed his eyes, as if that made zero sense. "What do you have to do?"

"I'm going to look into getting some sort of job around here. If everyone views me as just a freeloader, it'll build resentment. Also, I don't think just hanging around and using up resources without contributing is a good idea. It's not healthy, and I'm sure there's no end to what needs to be done around here now." We'd lost a couple centuries in technology. There would be plenty of jobs to do. They might be happy to have me.

"You're asking a group of people who already don't like humans to give you a job? That might not be a smart move." All hints of the flirty Duncan I'd seen were long gone now. He was back to looking at me like I was crazy.

"I'll be fine. I just have to track down Groza while you go

fishing." Even saying that woman's name made me want to shiver. I didn't imagine my reception was going to be any warmer today, but I had to start somewhere. Until I had a better plan in place, this was it for us.

"Don't go to Groza. Catarina is the one around here who handles those things, and it's better that way." He leaned slightly closer, his jaw clenched. "You need to watch yourself around here. This is not my pack."

"I watch *everywhere*." I had been for a while now. It was the only reason I was still alive, and the last place I was going to let my guard down was here, surrounded by monsters.

———

Every person I passed glanced my way, but no one said a word as I made my way to Catarina's. Jaysa, the spooky lady all in black, was watching me from her stoop again, sending a prickling feeling down my spine. I picked up my pace, hoping she'd either lose interest or sight of me. Either would do.

Catarina's door was open, and an older woman, who I presumed was Catarina, was sitting behind a desk. Salt-and-pepper hair was pulled back tight, accenting high cheekbones.

"Don't linger outside. I don't like skulkers." Her words were clipped and matter-of-fact, but she had the directness of someone who spoke to everyone the same way. As long as she was equally brusque across the board, I was fine with it.

I walked into the small cabin. "For the record, I wasn't skulking. I was debating whether I should knock because your door was already open, but I didn't want to be rude and walk in, either." Now I was rambling. I couldn't have just walked in?

She glanced at the door and then shrugged, as if conceding

me the point. She gave me a long once-over before she motioned to the chair. "Sit."

I did as she said, not looking to make more enemies than needed. The deck was already stacked against me.

"You're the new human who showed up with Duncan's pack yesterday."

I nodded, even though it hadn't been a question. This group didn't look like it had seen too many humans. So much for any delusion of blending. Even though I couldn't tell a shifter from a human, *they* all seemed to know instantly.

"What did you come to see me for?" she asked.

"I heard you're the one who works out the duties and jobs around this place. I figured I might be of use while I'm here." I folded my hands in my lap and tried to assume my interview pose.

She looked up again, giving a slight nod. I might've been taken off the *complete waste of life* list, but she wasn't jumping up and down, either.

"What can you do?" she asked, pencil hovering.

"I'm not trained in a lot of the skills you might need, but I'm a quick learner." Seriously, though, how many people still knew how to milk a cow?

She rolled her eyes at that and then let out a loud breath. She grabbed another book and flipped through the pages.

"Groza isn't a fan of humans," she said. "She'd want me to put you on latrines if she knew you were here."

Panic shot through me. Whatever she gave me, I'd have to take it, and damned if I'd say a word to Duncan about what I was doing.

She laughed. "Don't look so green. I like to keep those jobs in my pocket for the people who piss me off. Being human doesn't upset me the way it seems to anger others. I mean, you can't help it if you're born with a disability, right?" She lifted a shoulder, as if she were commiserating with me.

"Nope. I can't help it that I'm human." I shrugged, as if agreeing that I was completely inept. I'd never considered being human a disability, but I really didn't want to mop pee all day. There was no point in arguing anyway. The best way to prove I was useful was to *show* I was useful.

She looked back to her list, scanning it. "Let's see what we can do. I don't want to send you out of the community. That's asking for trouble. Way too easy for someone to pick you off in the woods, and then your people would come blaming me when you disappeared."

She kept going through her list as those little tidbits sank in. They'd kill me in the forest? Duncan and his guys were *my* people?

"You don't look sturdy enough for most manual labor jobs. Can you cook at all?" she asked.

"I make really good ramen noodles, and I can fry eggs and stuff."

She raised her eyebrows. "So that's a no. You're not making this easy on me, that's for sure." She let out another long breath. "Okay, I'm going to put you on errands. I'm not sure what kind yet, since I'm making this job up for you, so it might change day to day. We'll figure it out because you seem like a decent enough kid." She leaned back and waited.

"Thank you. Thank you so very much."

She nodded and smiled. "You are a quick learner. Don't piss me off and you won't be scrubbing piss, okay?"

"Got it. Not going to be a problem. What should I do today?"

"I don't have time to figure that out at the moment, so I'd take today as a freebie," she said.

"Then you won't hear from me until tomorrow." There was no way I was going to argue with her.

She nodded and waved her hand toward the door, as if she'd wasted enough time on me for the day. That was fine by me.

I made my way back to the cottage, afraid to linger around the town area and tempt fate, especially after what Catarina had said about disappearing into the woods.

As I walked briskly, Jaysa walked out of her door and onto her stoop, as if she'd been watching for me. I kept my eyes forward, not daring to look her way for more than a second. If there was one person in this place that set me on edge more than Groza, it was her, and she hadn't said a word to me.

The cottage was empty. I was completely alone. It was the first time I'd had more than a few minutes by myself in weeks. I went upstairs, took Charlie's items, and fixed him a drawer in the dresser before heading back downstairs to go through the rest of the supplies. That was when the floor beneath me dropped out.

I'd lined up all of Charlie's insulin. I'd planned on taking inventory, get a count on how much I had and when I'd need to get more. I was gripping the edge of the kitchen table, keeping as calm as possible, when Charlie walked in.

"Why is my medicine all lined up?" Charlie asked.

"Oh, I was just organizing." I rubbed the top of his head. "How was fishing?"

"I caught a huge bass! Duncan said it was the biggest first catch he'd ever seen. It was, like, this big." He held his arms outstretched.

Duncan walked in after him, took a look at the bottles and my strained expression, and turned to Charlie. "You should go next door and take Buddie your catch. He's going to show you how to clean it."

Charlie glanced at me. As soon as I nodded, he took off like a bat out of hell. Only a five-year-old would be enthused about gutting a fish.

"What's wrong?" Duncan said.

"Look at them." I waved my hand, having a hard time getting past the constriction in my throat to verbalize the problem.

He held up a couple vials and then a few more. "Some of them are cloudy," he said, as if sensing that was the issue.

"They should be clear. It means they're going bad."

He put them down, staring at them. "How much time left on them, do you think?" he asked.

"Couple weeks if I'm really careful and don't let him so much as look at a sweet, and that's if the rest don't go bad soon."

He was standing so close I could feel the heat of his body, and all I wanted at that moment was to just collapse into him. He'd take control and try to handle it all, because that was what he did. That was the type of person he was. I'd gone from resenting pancakes this morning to being as bad as Charlie, looking at Duncan like he was the cure to all ills.

My stomach roiled, and I braced my hands on the table. Then I forced myself to the other side, putting space between us. I sank into a chair and then bent over, not caring how I looked. I was going to look a lot worse if I threw up, which was about to happen.

I couldn't fall apart. I had to hold it together. *Breathe in, hold, breathe out.* Duncan didn't say anything but waited until I leaned back in my chair.

"You okay?" he said.

"It depends. Do they have any insulin here?"

He shook his head. "I already looked into it. Shifters don't get diabetes, and they have a different attitude toward things. I like to have a stash of items to barter with. Groza's pack is more of a 'take what you need' kind of group. But there's a place not that far from here that might have some."

"How do you know?" I asked, as a glimmer of hope ignited in my chest.

"I already inquired, knowing that this was going to be an issue at some point."

He stared at the insulin while I stared at him. He'd already been preparing? He did that for us? For Charlie?

"Where? Can we go there now?" I said.

"I can't, but you can. It actually has the added benefit of serving a purpose to Groza. It's a group of scientists and doctors running a food and health clinic of sorts. She wants them checked out."

"So it buys me some good graces at the same time as possibly locating a supply?" Figured Groza would be skeptical of do-gooders. The world had fallen apart, and she couldn't understand why anyone would help others.

"Yes. If you're serving a purpose, Groza is going to be more welcoming, and the pack will follow her lead."

"When can I go?" I didn't care if this would ingratiate me to the pack. That concern had dropped to the bottom of my list once I saw the insulin was going bad. If it helped Groza, fine. If it didn't, that didn't matter either.

"I'm working on it now, but in the next couple of days."

Chapter Twenty-Two

"WHY ARE WE EATING THIS?" Charlie lifted up his spoon, and the oatmeal poured off and then fell in a brownish clump. It was a little charred here and there, and the water I'd added after the fact didn't seem to have helped matters.

Duncan claimed he was letting his cool, although I had a feeling it was going to never be cool enough.

"It's oatmeal. It's good for you." I wasn't much of a cook before the apocalypse, and now I was trying to function on a wood stove. Still, it wasn't like I was poisoning Charlie. There was going to be a learning curve. Although I might take pity on us all and accidentally sleep in a little later tomorrow.

"It doesn't look like oatmeal, and it tastes funny." He dropped his spoon back in the bowl and then stared at me, almost accusatorily.

"Eat it. It's good for you, and you need something in your stomach before you go to school."

Duncan had told me this morning that Charlie was welcome to attend. No one shifted until their teens, and there wouldn't be much difference between him and the other kids.

That hadn't made me completely comfortable, and I had every intention of spying on the class throughout the day.

"I can't believe I still have to go to school." Charlie's head was slumped as he tried to eat his oatmeal.

"You're going to like it. You'll make friends. It'll be fun." *Please, let it be fun.* He needed to run around with kids and be young. I didn't want him sitting around here watching me stress over the end of the world every day.

"I *have* friends," he said.

He'd *had* friends. Even if we were still in New York his school friends were all dead, that included the friends who'd been in our building.

"You don't have any here," I said.

"Come on. I'll walk you over and show you a cool surprise on the way," Duncan said, getting up and urging him along.

Charlie's face lit at Duncan's offer. It was better for them to see him with Duncan. It might help smooth the way for him with the teacher and other kids. Still, something in me tensed. It was just going to make things harder, because it wasn't like we could make a life here long term. It didn't even seem like Duncan was trying to prepare Charlie for the day when he'd no longer be in the kid's life. Why did it have to be so easy between them?

But it was better while we were here that he liked Duncan. I just wished he liked him a little less.

"Can we go fishing tomorrow?" Charlie asked as they got ready to leave, not even looking for my approval anymore.

It was his first day of school in a place that put me on edge. Nothing would probably make me happy this morning.

"I don't know about tomorrow, but definitely next week. Come on," Duncan said, heading out with him.

. . .

I headed over to Catarina's, still catching stares but not quite as many or as long as I had yesterday. Baby steps. If it kept trending in the right direction, maybe we'd be able to stay a little longer than I'd thought. I nearly jogged past Jaysa's cabin, but on cue, she walked onto her stoop right as I neared. She was one hundred percent watching for me.

I made it to Catarina's in record time. The door was open again, and I didn't linger on the stoop.

"I'm here for work," I said, smiling as if I were optimistic, which I wasn't. One wrong move could land me on latrine duty.

"Rastin blocked you out for an hour. You need to meet him over at the last cabin on the right on Percy Lane." She motioned to the left.

"I know which way that is. Did he say why?" Why wouldn't he have just asked me if he needed something? I was right next door to him. Why was I meeting him at some other cottage?

"Of course he didn't." She looked up, probably because I wasn't moving. "Is there a problem?"

"No. I'm on it." I forced myself to move, following the directions she'd given me.

What in the hell did Rastin want? No matter what he was looking for, it couldn't be sex. The guy hated me. I hadn't once picked up on a sexual vibe from him. He'd never given me as much as a cursory once-over to see what I was packing. I'd be less surprised if he was trying to off me.

Oh no. Was that it? Was he trying to kill me?

I got to the cottage and then froze on the porch. He must've been watching for me from the window, because the door swung open.

"Come in before anyone sees you." He reached out and

pulled me in. "Why do you smell like you're expecting me to eat you?" he said as soon as the door was shut.

"No I don't." I probably did, but I wasn't giving him any ideas. Was there a smell for that?

Why wasn't he dressed? Why was he in a robe? Did he want sex? Was he one of those weirdos who liked to sleep with women he hated? I was not sleeping with Rastin.

"What is this about? Where are we? Whose house is this?" I asked, backing away from him and checking out possible exits.

"They save it for guests." He walked past me, not tracking my movements like a predator would. He wasn't acting like he wanted sex. He seemed annoyed that I was here at all. Nothing about this scenario felt normal.

"I need help with this stuff, but if you tell anyone what we're doing, I *will* eat you." He pointed to a bunch of boxes on the table.

It was like he'd wiped out the beauty department of the nearest big-box store: eyebrow cream, razors, and lotion, to name a few. He even had a few tubs of hot wax, and I didn't think it was for kinky sex.

"What exactly is it you need from me?" I sorted through more items. Tweezers! I needed a pair of those desperately.

"There are no salons left, and I have certain standards that need to be upheld." He lifted his chin, as if to show off his superior jaw line.

I held up a box. "You want me to wax you?"

"Yes. And nails, too." He held his hands out. "Nothing too flashy. Just my cuticles trimmed up and maybe buffed to a nice shine."

"You know I'm not a beautician, right?" Kicking him in

the balls might be a preferable afternoon when the other choice was grooming him.

"Yes, but you also look like one of those poor humans that used this over-the-counter crap," he said in pure Rastin form, once again highlighting why he wasn't exactly my favorite shifter.

He was right, though. I was familiar with more than one of these items. But still, why me? Because there was no one else?

"You're saying none of the people around here can do this for you?"

"I can't have everyone knowing what I do to look good. They think it's natural. I have a reputation." He probably had a reputation, all right, but not what he thought it was.

I eyed up his stash. "If I do this, I have a price."

"Letting you breathe was the price. Carrying you around on my back through the woods and through a river was the price," he said, planting his hands on his hips.

I noticed then that he didn't have on shoes. He better not think I was touching those toenails.

"I want supplies, mostly razors. I prefer the kind with the three blades and a moisturizing strip, but I'll take whatever you've got." I wasn't as high maintenance as he was, but a steady supply of razors would be a luxury out here.

He started flipping his head around.

I ignored his false outrage, knowing it was a bargaining tactic, and waited him out. It didn't take long.

"Fine. Now let's get to work. I've got a date tonight, and I'm in rough shape." He turned, giving me his back and lowering his robe. It was a good thing he was facing away from me, because the forest growing on his back was jaw-dropping.

He turned his profile to me. "Well?" he said.

"I can fix this. It might take more than an hour, though." I looked at his back from a different angle. This shit was *thick*. "We might not get to the nails today. I'm going to need some scissors or a trimmer first, and we might need more containers of wax."

"But you got this?"

"I got this." For feminine and beauty products in the apocalypse? I'd tackle much worse than this forest.

"We don't have a microwave, but I've got a pot boiling on the wood stove," he said.

He waved me in the direction as if this were all on me. For razors, I'd do it.

I caught Rastin looking at me almost contemplatively as I melted wax. "What?" I said.

"Nothing." He shrugged.

I wasn't pulling it out of him. I went back to poking the wax.

"How are you and Duncan doing over in the cottage together?" he asked a minute later.

"Fine. We don't get along that well, but we're both adults." What did he think we'd do? Have death matches every night? I poked at the wax again, trying to get it to melt faster.

"He keeps tabs on wherever you are," he said, watching me like he didn't want to miss a single blink or exhale.

"Yeah, well, he's bossy like that," I said. *Dammit, wax. Melt already.* "Let's start weed-whacking that mess while this melts," I said, hoping to move him off more talk of Duncan.

He had batteries for the trimmer I used, which made it harder to talk. Then he was too busy whining as I tortured him with wax that was too hot.

Two hours later, Rastin held up a mirror while he had me

hold another behind him. "It doesn't look as good as my girl at the salon, but I guess it's okay."

"Then go back to your salon girl," I said, dropping the mirror.

"I can't. She's dead." His tone sounded closer to self-pity than that of someone in mourning.

"My point exactly. You're lucky anyone is willing to battle that forest on your back. I'm surprised the missing link didn't crawl out of it while I was chopping it down." I walked over to the table, plucking up some razors and a pair of tweezers. "My pay, thank you very much."

"Hey, do me a favor and wash up as soon as you get back to the cottage," he said as I headed to the door..

"Why? I'm not dirty." I'd been very careful to steer clear of the demolition as I worked.

"Just, you know, scrub up a bit. Maybe change your shirt." He made a little circle with his finger.

I glanced down, looking for wax but not finding any. "Yeah, sure."

I left the cottage and then swung past the school. I hadn't stopped worrying about Charlie since he'd left this morning. I ducked behind a building and spotted him kicking a ball around with some other kids, laughing and yelling. Things definitely looked as if they were going well.

I made my way back to the cottage, deciding that changing might not be the worst idea. What if there was something about Rastin's hair that would cause a rash and he didn't want to tell me? He was a monster, after all.

Duncan walked in a minute or so after me, before I'd had time to go upstairs, lines forming on his forehead.

"I spoke to Groza. We're going to the clinic tomorrow," he said.

He walked into the kitchen where I'd stopped to check on the insulin yet again. I'd stared at the vials so many times at this point that I wasn't sure if they were getting cloudier or if I was becoming more paranoid.

"That's great."

His brow furrowed deeper as he came closer. "You smell different. Why do you smell like that?" He was full-on scowling now. "What did you do today?"

"I don't know. Errands. Would you like a list of everything I did?" I had no intention of telling him anything that had happened. I'd agreed to a keep silent. Plus I didn't want my supplies cut off. But he was still staring at me like I might've gone off and murdered someone today. "I had to help with some laundry and stuff," I said, trying to throw him off the scent, literally.

"Rastin's laundry?" he asked. His voice had a weird reverberation to it as he pronounced *Rastin*.

"Yes. I had to help Rastin. It wasn't how I wanted to spend my day, because he annoys me, but there it is." The details might've been skewed, but my annoyance was underplayed, if anything. There was definitely a reason Rastin had told me to change. He better not have given me anything weird, or he was going to have to find a new landscaper for his back. "Can you tell me more about the clinic? What do I need to do?"

Duncan watched me for another moment and then the scowl smoothed. "Just get in and try to take a look around, get a feel for the place."

"Why does Groza care about this place so much? Have they bothered her at all?" I asked.

"There's murmurs that this clinic might be testing bodies of the dead, running tissue samples against the living. Plus,

Groza's not a trusting sort." His eyes narrowed as he added that last part, as if he were reminding me never to forget it.

"Do you think they might know something about what happened?" I'd given up on finding out. I thought everyone had. I'd figured that the ability to perform complex scientific experiments died the day all the people had.

"If they do know something, I doubt they'll tell you anyway. This is more of a headcount and security rundown trip." He moved about the kitchen, checking supplies, as he threw out this information like it meant nothing.

"Wait, am I casing the place for her? Because I'm not okay with that."

He stopped what he was doing. "What if that's the only way you can get insulin? You do realize they probably aren't going to be willing to hand over whatever you ask for, right? Are you saying you wouldn't do it for him?"

Talk about hitting a sore target. I slumped back against the counter. Was this the cost of surviving? It might be the cost for Charlie, and there was no price I wasn't willing to pay. He was just a boy, and he deserved to make it to being a man, even if the price was my soul.

Yeah, Duncan was right. I'd do it. I'd crawl through a swamp to keep Charlie alive—but that didn't mean I was going to enjoy it.

"Get your head right before we leave tomorrow or you aren't going," he said.

Every single time I started softening toward him, he turned into *this*.

"My head is fine. I have some morals still left intact. Sorry if that bothers you." My eyes shot to his.

"You think you're the first person to make compromises? First person even in this room? That's what you do when other people's lives depend on you. If you think I'll let you walk in there looking like a martyr, you're wrong."

He might be correct, but that didn't make it right. Or good. Or help make this world better. None of that mattered, because Charlie needed insulin.

"Don't tell me you will or won't let me do this. I'll be going with or without you, even if I have to talk to Groza myself." I straightened, taking a step toward him, ready to knee him in the balls if that was what it took.

The angrier I got, the calmer he seemed to grow. "As long as you walk in like this and not the girl who was moping a few seconds ago."

"Don't take this the wrong way, but sometimes all I want to do is punch you," I said, getting in his space. "I really don't like you most of the time."

"I'd rather have you punch me than shake in fear."

Neither of us moved, and that strange tension between us grew.

I reached out and pushed him, telling myself it was because I wanted to punch him but was holding back. That it didn't have anything to do with wanting to touch him.

I did it again, and this time he caught my hand, holding it and not letting go. The heat in his eyes didn't look like anger. It warmed and loosened the knot that I always seemed to carry around in my stomach these days.

"I'm home!" Charlie called, skipping in the door with Buddie.

I shot to the other side of the kitchen, telling myself we hadn't been about to kiss. Duncan was still standing where he'd been, the heat in his eyes calling me a liar.

Chapter Twenty-Three

DUNCAN WAS WAITING downstairs for me the next morning.

"Are you ready?" he asked.

"Yep." There wasn't much to get ready for. I'd go to the clinic and try to figure out whether they had insulin. All the while I'd case the place for Groza in case she wanted to burn it to the ground to appease her paranoia. I wasn't sure what that made me: desperate or despicable. It was probably a check in both columns. They didn't seem to be exclusive.

Sure, I could stand here and rationalize that the people running the clinic probably hoarded the food they were now doling out. Groza's intel about their running experiments and testing made them bad people, and they deserved whatever they got. None of that was working, though. I was a little too self-aware to buy into it, even if I wanted to. I knew that I'd be right there beside Groza, giving her the gasoline if they had insulin and didn't hand it over. When it came to Charlie, I was ready to crawl through the slimiest of swamps.

Easy times had allowed me the illusion that I was a better person than I seemed. Times like this stripped that all away. I was learning that I was willing to become the worst kind of human if it meant that Charlie would survive.

Duncan leaned an arm against the banister, watching me. "You good?" He eyed me up like he could read my mind and was ready to block the door if I wasn't mentally right with what I was doing.

"I said I'm ready." It was one thing to come to terms with what I was becoming and a whole other thing to admit it to him, someone I didn't trust and usually didn't like.

Buddie was outside, talking to Trevor and Rastin.

"I need a minute with Buddie before we leave," I said, meeting Buddie's gaze and tilting my head to the side.

"What's wrong?" he asked, following me over.

Buddie wasn't coming with us for one reason: I'd insisted he stay behind. Charlie had gone to school again today, but I wanted someone I trusted to stay with him. Buddie was the closest I had.

"If something were to happen to me today, would you take care of Charlie? Like, *really* take care of him? I don't know how things work with your kind, but humans need a lot of help for a long while."

He shook his head. "Nothing is going to happen to you. This is just—"

"We don't know that. We don't know anything anymore." Had Death Day taught him nothing? You couldn't depend on the next minute, let alone the next day.

"Of course I'll do it."

"You promise? You'll take care of him like he's your own? I need to hear you say it."

"Yes." He might've answered begrudgingly, but he meant it.

"Thank you." There would be someone there for my brother if something happened to me. I couldn't completely shake the fear of leaving Charlie, but it took the edge off.

"Now stop thinking like that, because that's not how you go into a job." Buddie was getting all grumpy, but it was better than Duncan, who got flat-out angry.

"I'm good." I was going to have to get a sign for these people soon, declaring myself okay with being morally gray from here on out. Otherwise I was going to have to keep rehashing these conversations.

There was a garage right outside the development where Groza was waiting beside two ATVs.

She pulled Duncan over to the side, speaking to him while glaring at me suspiciously. Did she think I'd become a double agent or something? Would it happen if that was the price of insulin?

I wasn't going to think like that yet. I'd just adjusted to morally gray. That felt like it was getting maybe a little too close to a blackened soul.

We were off pretty quickly, as Duncan hadn't seemed to want to waste too much time talking to her.

About an hour or so later, we pulled up to the outskirts of the small town where the clinic was located. Apparently being within a certain mile radius was enough to put it on Groza's shit list. No other reason needed.

"You're going to have to walk the next few blocks, but I'll be watching you," Duncan said. "You won't be truly alone until you're in the clinic."

"I got it." I climbed out of the ATV.

Duncan grabbed my arm, stopping me when I would've left. "Listen to me," he said. "You don't eat anything; you don't let them take anything from you. You get information and get out."

"I got it." I yanked my arm away, hating the sizzle of awareness that shot through me anytime we touched, and even more so now. I had a job to go do, unsuspecting people to screw. I didn't have time to regress to a teenybopper with hormones flaming out of control.

I walked toward my destination, trying to put Duncan out of my head.

It didn't take long to find "free meals" signs with arrows painted in broad strokes, pointing the way. The closer I got, the more people I saw milling about. I did a mental count, again confirming what he'd said about more men being left than women. It hadn't seemed to be that way with the shifters, but they'd also fared much better in general.

I walked closer to the building and got in the line formed at the door.

"They really give food here?" I asked the guy in front of me when he looked over his shoulder.

"Yeah. I've been coming here every day. You new to the neighborhood?" He smiled, and I suddenly regretted opening up a conversation with the way he was eyeing me.

"Yeah. My brothers and I just moved here. They're supposed to be meeting me here any minute. It was nothing short of a miracle all eight of us survived."

He nodded, his smile losing some of its glow, before turning back around. Guess he didn't feel like small talk anymore.

I caught a flash of a movement on the roof. Did they have

snipers up there? As if they'd noticed my attention, a man all in black walked to the edge of the roof, his gun in his hand. Another one joined him. Okay, so I hadn't expected *that*, but they were giving out food. They probably had to have security. It didn't make them evil.

The door opened, and a middle-aged woman in a white jacket, with sharp eyes, scanned the crowd. She paused on me for a second before she stepped to the side and said, "Come on in, John," to the man next in line.

"They take us one at a time?" I asked the guy in front of me.

"Yes, but the line moves pretty fast." He didn't bother turning around this time.

"They can't just hand out bags? You know, like a soup kitchen?"

"No. They're scientists. In return for the meal, you have to give them some samples. They're trying to figure out why some people survived when most didn't." He was answering my questions but acting as if it were a chore.

"Where'd they get all the food?" I pressed, even though he clearly didn't want to talk to me anymore. I should've held off on the brother story.

"I don't know," he said. His words were growing more clipped. "Some people say that they were part of the army, or some branch of government. I don't care as long as they share it."

I fell silent as we moved closer. I hadn't made it in the building yet. Getting caught snooping wouldn't be a good look.

The guy turned out to be correct. It didn't take long for the line to dwindle, only another twenty minutes or so.

The same middle-aged woman opened the door, waving me in. She smiled as she shut the door. "I'm Abigail. I haven't seen you before. Is this your first time?"

"Yes." I looked around the halls, which were all white, and the place smelled slightly of bleach and disinfectant. I could see why everyone referred to it as "the clinic." There was a hum of other voices, but all the doors were shut.

"Well, this is how things work. We'll give you a hot meal, and in return, we would appreciate it if you could give us some samples. You know, just standard hair, mouth swabs, and such?" Her tone was pleasant and upbeat.

I had a feeling "and such" was blood, tissue, and everything else that might make a person a little distrusting.

"Do I have to give samples of everything? I'm a little squeamish." I'd ripped off the tip of my finger in my teens. I hadn't even blanched, but they didn't know that.

"I'm not sure if you've heard about us, but we're a group of scientists trying to find the cause of Death Day. We want to help make sure it never happens again, but we can't do it alone. Samples are appreciated but not strictly enforced." She spoke to me like a teacher I'd had in first grade, preaching about good manners.

She was a little bit more effective, though. Talk about a guilt trip. "Could I only do the hair this time?"

"Sure. We can start slow. And we might not need any samples from you as you come more often. It depends on what leads we're following."

"Okay." It really didn't sound like an outlandish request.

She pointed to a room off to the side as if we'd come to some sort of agreement. I wasn't sure what it was, though, as I walked into a sterile room that looked like a doctor's office. It had an exam bench on the side but also a table and chairs.

"As you eat, I'm just going to take down a basic medical history, if you don't mind," she said, going to the table.

"Sure."

She started running through a list of questions I would've answered at any doctor's appointment, nothing that raised any kind of alarm. A few seconds later, there was a knock at the door. A young man carried in a food tray with two slices of pizza and a can of soda.

Pizza. *Thin-sliced* pizza. This wasn't your run-of-the-mill freezer slices. This stuff looked legitimate, like they might be harboring a pizza oven here. If I was going to let them take the samples, why *shouldn't* I get the payoff? Screw this no-eating business.

"Could I take a swab from your mouth before you start?"

I had the slice almost to my mouth when she asked. How was I supposed to say no? "Sure."

She was quick and efficient. It was such a nothing that I wasn't sure what everyone's issue was. I was tearing into the pizza and not regretting a thing. She continued questioning me as I ate, jotting down notes about my weight, height, age, etc. Then she hit me with a question I should've been ready for but wasn't.

"Surviving family? They don't have to be alive now, but did you have relatives who survived Death Day?"

"My father," I said, knowing I'd stiffened.

"And is he still alive?"

It hadn't been that long. Odds were he was. "I'm not sure. I haven't seen him in a few weeks. I don't know what happened to him."

"Any other living relatives?" She watched me as if my initial reaction had gotten her antenna up.

"No." The second I said it, I knew it had come out a tad harsh, and I'd given away another hint I was lying. There was no way she'd missed it, not the way she glanced over her glasses at me. "I'm sorry. It's just that… Well, I have no one. I'm still processing," I added, trying to give her a reason to hang her hat on.

She smiled. "I understand."

Her poker face was way better than mine. I couldn't tell if I'd sold her or not.

I went back to eating my pizza, and she came closer with a small bag and scissors. "We need about twenty strands or so. Do you care where I take the sample from?"

How did I not give her hair? What was the difference, anyway? It couldn't be as bad as the mouth swab.

"Underneath, if you don't mind." Less likely Duncan would notice that way.

"Do you care if I save the crusts for later?"

"Not at all. Tomorrow is meatloaf and mashed potatoes," she said, smiling and handing me the soda. Now that she had her questions answered and her samples, it felt like I was about to get the bum's rush.

She opened the door, but I wasn't budging from my spot.

"Before I go, I have a friend who has diabetes. Is there any way you can help them here? Any kind of medications? They aren't in bad shape, but they do need some insulin. Do you have any?"

"We might be able to give them some. You should have them come with you."

My body felt like it wanted to seize at the suggestion of bringing Charlie here. Was I being overprotective? They seemed nice enough, but a little too… I couldn't put my finger on it. I just didn't want to bring him here, and wouldn't unless I ran out of every other option possible.

"I'm not sure they can make the trip. Is there another option?" I gripped the chair. I'd be holding on to the doorjamb next if she tried to make me leave without giving me the right answer.

She gave me a long once-over, as if weighing my value. It was worse than the look I got from the guy in line.

"We can probably figure out something. We'll talk next time you come."

I left without her having to call security. I didn't breathe easy until I got out of there, but my trust-meter had gone into negative numbers since Death Day. I couldn't tell if it was them or my paranoia.

There was the feeling of someone following me on my way back, but this time I was getting stalked by monsters I knew. Duncan fell into step with me as I neared the ATVs.

He looked at me as if he had some knowledge of my transgressions and that I hadn't followed most of his instructions. Even if I hadn't, he didn't know that, no matter how special he thought he was.

"How many things did you do that you weren't supposed to? Exact number," Duncan asked as we climbed into the ATVs.

I pulled the crust out of my pocket. "I got you your food sample, as requested."

He took it from me and held it up. "That you *ate*. Why is it you can't follow instructions?"

"It was *pizza*." That was all he should need to know.

He shook his head. "What did you see?"

"Not that much." I gave him the rundown of the hallway and the room, knowing the trip had been a bust. There was always tomorrow.

I pulled the can of soda out of my pocket, cracked it open, and took a sip.

Duncan made growling noises.

"What? It was factory sealed." At least he didn't know about the hair and the mouth swab.

Chapter Twenty-Four

I WALKED into Caterina's office and dropped into a chair.

"How'd the clinic go yesterday?"

"Good. I think we're going back tomorrow." I'd wanted to go today but was overruled. They didn't have a kid who needed insulin, so it was easy for them to drag this out. "They seem like maybe they just want to help people."

Catarina leaned forward on her elbows, lowering her chin. "But something in your gut is bothering you?"

"No." I shrugged. "I mean, not really. There wasn't anything that screamed *problem*."

She was staring at me with such a determined gaze that more words started spewing out.

"There's something I can't put my finger on niggling away at my brain." It was probably seeing snipers on the roof of a clinic. That would throw anyone.

"They're on Groza's radar for some reason. She might be a bitch, but she's got the best gut of anyone I ever met. If her antenna is up, never dismiss it out of hand." She pointed at me, as if to make sure I was taking a mental note.

I was still reeling over the fact that she'd called Groza a bitch when she said, "Anyway, she told me to send you over to her place. She wants to talk to you."

"Groza wants me? Why?" The last thing I wanted to do today was spend time with that woman.

"She didn't say, and I didn't ask. Just head over to Fred's Mercantile in the main square, make a left, and go to Martha's House."

She pulled out one of the maps from the visitors' center and pointed at the cartoon representation of a cute little white colonial.

"You need this?" she said, holding out the paper.

"No. I've got it."

"Good. Eventually we're going to run out of these, and I like having some on hand." She tucked it back into a drawer.

I walked through the town, and people stared a little less than they had yesterday. Another few days and they might not look at all. I mean, maybe no one would ever speak to me, but I was good with being ignored.

There was something nice about all these handy signs marking the buildings. I found Martha's House easily. It wasn't a surprise Groza took this place, with its gingerbread trim and rocking chairs on the porch. It vomited up charm everywhere you looked. It wasn't huge, but it was twice the size of Bunny's Cottage.

I rang the bell, which was some antique iron ball-and-cup ordeal hanging beside the door with a rope.

"Come in," she yelled. "I'm in the kitchen."

The inside was warm and inviting, which was the exact opposite of the vibe Groza gave off. Actually, I might've been a hair surprised she chose this place.

"You wanted to see me?"

"Yes. Thank you for coming."

There it was again, that thing I'd sensed from her. She wasn't outright attacking me, but there was this underlying feeling that if we were standing at the edge of a cliff, she'd reach out and push me to my death in a cool and calculated way. Although she needed me right now for the clinic. Perhaps she brought me here to torture me?

"Why don't you take a seat? I've got some coffee brewing if you'd like," she said. The corners of her mouth seemed to be struggling to rise but couldn't quite make the feat.

"Coffee?" She could ram a wedge of wood under my nail if she was going to do it after coffee.

She poured me a cup and then put both sugar and cream on the table.

I eyed up both. Wow. She was laying it on thick.

"We're getting pretty self-sufficient at this point," she said, as if it weren't that big of a deal. She sat down opposite me, drinking her coffee black. She would, too. That was just the kind of chick she looked like. Black coffee, whisky straight, and she probably fucked like a demon out of hell. I tried to eye up her hands. I bet she had calluses on her palms a foot thick and hadn't noticed the pain when she earned them. She was all the things I wanted to be when I grew up.

Unfortunately, I was already an adult. I just didn't feel like that sitting across from her.

"What did you make of the clinic?" she said.

Okay, maybe this was why I was here. She was one of those people who liked to hear things firsthand. No big deal. I could respect that.

"It seemed normal enough." I was going to leave it at that, but then I added, "Except something has been bothering me all today and I can't put my finger on it." I didn't want to encourage her to attack the place, but if they were a threat? I was living here with Charlie. A threat to them was now a threat to him.

She watched me intently as I spoke. "That's my feeling as well."

"You're aware of what I need from the place?" I knew Duncan had talked to her about the insulin, but she wasn't the only one who liked to hear things firsthand.

"Yes. If we take the place down, which I'm suspecting we might have to, whatever insulin supplies they have are yours."

"Thank you." Maybe she wasn't as horrible as I'd thought? She seemed pretty easy to deal with at the moment. Had I been anticipating a problem to the point I'd created one in my head? She was just a stressed-out alpha, doing her job, trying to keep her people safe. It was probably hard running a pack like this.

"That's not the only reason I wanted you to come by," she said. "I like to lay things out on the table whenever possible, so I thought it would be good to clear the air."

Okay, maybe it wasn't *all* in my head. Clearing the air wasn't needed unless something had stunk it up. The coffee had been a trap to butter me up.

Talking about buttering me up—if this was going to be really bad, she could've thrown in a couple buttered biscuits, maybe a cookie or two, to fatten me up so I was sluggish for the fight.

"Sure. That's probably a good idea." It might be better to know how I'd already pissed her off. Considering this was the most we'd conversed so far, I had a feeling I wouldn't be able to fix it. It was hard to cease breathing unless I killed myself.

She put her coffee cup down, and even though I'd finished mine, she hadn't offered me a refill.

"Times are pretty uncertain at the moment," she said.

"There's safety in numbers. The more loyalty within those numbers, the better."

"Yes, I think I understand. I might be human, but I can tell you, I'm not a disloyal person if you're concerned about that. I would do whatever I could to help those who've helped me."

She smiled like I was a young pup, too naïve to understand what she was saying.

"As wonderful as that is to hear, and I do appreciate the thought, I wasn't overly concerned about your loyalty."

Her tone was so condescending that it was hard not to tell her to go screw and walk out of here. But I wouldn't, because she'd just promised me the insulin from the clinic I couldn't raid on my own.

"Then what is the problem?" I asked, trying to keep the annoyance from my tone but knowing I was failing.

"I have plans to merge packs, mine and Duncan's. Times are uncertain, and I want solid numbers. I don't need any obstacles to that." The highlights in her eyes were shaped like daggers as she stared at me.

"How would I be an obstacle? That's between you and Duncan. I'd never presume to interfere, nor would I be able to." It wasn't like we were having heart-to-hearts every night, discussing plans for the future. As far as Duncan was concerned, I couldn't even make my own decisions well. What sway did she think I had?

"I don't think you're understanding. Pack mergers are rare because it's difficult for two alphas to cooperate. The only time it happens is when it's a mated male and female alpha."

Duncan hadn't seemed to care for her, and she was far from a woman in love. No, this was exactly what I'd expect from someone of her nature. It all made sense—except for me.

"Again, I'm not sure what this has to do with me. There is

nothing between us." If the insulin carrot wasn't still dangling, I would've already left.

"He's protective of you in a way that's not natural for a shifter toward a human. I don't particularly care if it's reciprocated or not. It's a *problem* for me."

"I don't see that, and I don't think it's a problem." If she thought I could cause any kind of disturbance, she'd get rid of me, and fast. The only thing saving me now was she needed me to case the clinic some more before they moved on it. She wouldn't kill me yet.

"If it's a problem, a solution will be found," she said, staring at me in a way that would give even the hardiest of people frostbite.

I had a feeling the solution would be a ditch in the woods.

"I think we're in a place of understanding," she said.

I nodded. She was brutally obvious.

She dismissed me with a nod.

Chapter Twenty-Five

THERE WERE four snipers on the roof of the clinic, or four that were visible. The windows all had bars. This place was locked down better than most banks. I made a point of looking at other nearby buildings, the way I was told, and caught the glint of the reflection off a scope in the nearest one next to it. A picture was forming, one bigger than just a group of doctors and scientists getting together on their own to help humanity.

"I'm glad to see you again," Abigail said as she waved me into the clinic. "I wasn't sure you were coming back after you missed yesterday."

"Sorry," I said, and then bent to tie my boot in the hall, the one I'd purposely left undone. It bought me a couple more seconds to gather more information, try to peek under door cracks.

She waved me into the same room as last time. "That friend I have with diabetes is really having a bad time of it. I was afraid to leave her. It's one of the reasons I made sure I came today. I was hoping you might have some of that insulin?"

Abigail leaned against the counter, holding her clipboard to her chest. "I spoke to my bosses about it. They said that they really need to save it for people we see in person. I mean, it might be different if we had a more established relationship with you, but…"

I still had *some* insulin. I didn't need to take rash actions—yet. But then there was Groza. There was a chance I'd be creeping out in the middle of the night. That woman was not someone I wanted to trifle with.

"What if I gave you some blood samples? Would you feel more comfortable giving me the insulin then?" They already had swabs, hair—what was the difference? Plus, what if they really were trying to get answers? Could I condemn them if they had also become morally gray, considering my own current attitudes?

She grinned. "We could probably work out something."

Duncan was going to kill me, and I didn't care. "So what's on the menu today? You guys don't have any cheesecake lying around, do you?" If I was going to do it, might as well make the most of it.

"I'll see what I can do." She smiled like the villain who'd turned the protagonist to the dark side.

———

"Why do you have a mark on your arm?" Duncan strode my way, intercepting me before I got to the ATVs. Birdie and Rastin didn't budge from theirs, knowing they didn't want any part of this fight.

"How can you see that?" There wasn't going to be any

denying it. He'd know as soon as he saw the vials of insulin that I must've given them something. He could be as pissed as he wanted, too. He wasn't responsible for Charlie's life.

"I asked, why do you have a mark on your arm?" He grabbed my wrist, holding my arm out and staring at me.

"I was asking them for some insulin. I had to play nice." I would've shrugged if my arm wasn't locked in place.

"So you let them stick a needle in you?" The veins in his neck were about to burst.

"I let them take a small blood sample, yes." I pulled away from him and continued walking to the ATV. "I knew you were going to overreact."

"This is done. You're not going back," he said as he followed me.

"If I have to let them hang me upside down and drain all my blood to get insulin, I'm doing it. It's not your call." I refused to look at him. I had no interest in arguing because I'd already made up my mind. Talking to him about it was a waste of time.

"You're my pack, and you're reckless. I say it's done, then it's done."

Birdie and Rastin watched on, speechless and mouths gaping open.

"Well, maybe I'll defect and become part of Groza's pack, and then it won't be any of your concern." I swung around. "And for the record, I'm not part of your pack. I'm a free agent. I'll go where I want."

"The fuck you will," he said.

"Yeah, I will," I replied, standing toe to toe with him.

I'd never seen him this angry, ever.

"Get in the ATV."

I tilted my head in that direction. "I *will* get in the ATV, but because I was about to get in it *anyway*. Not because you said so." I turned and grabbed the roll bar. "This is me getting in of my own free will, so we're clear on things."

Duncan walked to the other side, and I caught a glimpse of Rastin's face in the other ATV. He shook his head at me, like I was psychotic. I rolled my eyes. Rastin was all big, bad, and tough until it came to Duncan or a vat of hot wax. Then he squirmed like a little girl.

Rastin left a bigger gap than normal while trailing our ATV, as if we were going to explode and shoot off shrapnel. There wasn't even speaking going on, let alone shouting.

As soon as we got back, Duncan parked the ATV and left.

I turned to Birdie and Rastin. "He's being ridiculous," I said, and took a couple steps toward them.

"I'm not getting involved. You two hash it out," Rastin said, nearly running from me. Birdie was hot on his heels.

I turned to head to the cottage when it hit me that Duncan had walked in the direction of Groza's. That bastard was going straight to her and calling off the clinic runs. Damned if I'd let him. I started running in that direction, afraid he'd win the fight before I got there.

Duncan was standing with Groza on her porch, and they were yelling at each other. I didn't have to guess about what.

"No one here freeloads. She's not going to use our resources and do nothing," Groza said.

"She's not going back there," Duncan said.

They were both scowling, and it was unclear who might kill who first.

"She's not going to eat our food and not contribute." Groza pointed at Duncan's chest. "I need her to go to the clinic, and that's where she's going."

"No, she's not," he said, swatting her hand away.

"I want to go back to the clinic," I said, walking right up to them.

"She's not going back," Duncan said, not looking at me.

Groza glanced my way for the briefest of moments, but only to glare, as if this proved her point that I was a complication in her plans.

"If she agreed, then what is the issue?" she said. "If she's too weak to be useful, why did you bring her here in the first place? You should've left her to die."

I stepped closer. "What the hell? I went to that place and did everything you asked and—"

Her nostrils flared and then she raised her lip, as if something about me was physically repulsive to her. She took a step back, holding out her hand to ward me off. "She smells off."

"What do you mean?" I asked. "Now I stink? That's the issue?"

She took a few more steps back. "Shit. It's getting stronger."

Duncan came closer, and I realized he'd been upwind of me.

"Dammit. She's right." He cursed under his breath.

"Someone got matto into her." She shook her head and looked as if she wanted to punch me. "This is why I don't want fucking humans in my pack," Groza said, growling.

"What's matto? What are you talking about?" I reached out and gripped the porch railing, feeling a little woozy out of nowhere. As worried as I probably should've been, the first thing that came to mind was that Duncan was going to be right and I'd never live it down. A distant second was how sick I was going to get.

"Get her out of here now," Groza yelled.

"I'll handle this," Duncan snapped at her before wrapping

his arm around my waist and steering me away from her place.

"What's she talking about?" I asked as the shifters who'd gathered to watch the fireworks darted out of our way.

"You couldn't listen," he said. "You had to do it your way." People were giving us plenty of space, and I didn't know if it was me or Duncan's glaring.

"Before you yell at me more, can you please explain what's going on?" I said.

"How do you feel? Like crap? Like maybe you're coming down with the flu and it's hitting you like a ton of bricks?"

I *was* feeling incredibly tired. "Maybe. Why? Am I sick?"

"You'll live, but you'll make every shifter around you sick as hell, and some of the weaker ones could die if you get near them. I have to get you out of here until this passes."

"Wait. What about Charlie?" I went to turn around, and he turned me back toward the exit.

"It'll only be a night, and Buddie can watch him until we get back. Now come on. This isn't going to go over well, and I want you out of here before it becomes an even bigger spectacle."

How many of them had already witnessed the scene on her porch? I'd been too riled up to pay attention, but probably a half a dozen. Meaning that at least half the pack was going to be pissed along with Groza. Who was I kidding? The entire pack would probably hate me.

We walked out of the community with all eyes on us. Any progress I'd made the last few days was going to be long gone once word spread.

"Aren't you going to get sick being close to me?"

"No," he said in a clipped tone, herding me out of the community.

"Can't I quarantine in the cottage?" I said, looking over my shoulder.

"No." His replies were getting shorter and growlier.

We walked past the garages. "We're not taking an ATV?"

He said nothing, not looking at me. He was walking faster now, and a gap was forming in between us. He was annoyed. *Got it.*

"You're blaming the clinic, but you don't know that it was them. Maybe it's something that sporadically happens with humans?"

"It's a *bioweapon* designed for our kind. It doesn't just *happen.*" He shook his head.

"That doesn't even make sense. Why would a group of scientists go out of their way to poison a breed of monsters they don't know exists?" I yelled at him.

"You're making an awful lot of assumptions with that statement." He glanced back at me. "Keep up, because I'm not carrying you."

"Did I ask you to carry me?" I snapped.

We'd only made it another twenty minutes when I felt the full force of the exhaustion weighing down on me. I kept moving, but from sheer force of will alone. Duncan kept looking back, as if waiting for me to ask for help. It wasn't going to happen.

I finally stopped, leaning against a tree.

Duncan didn't go more than a few steps before he turned, waiting.

I glared his way. "I don't want your help. I'll catch up, but I'm not running so you can punish me."

He walked back to me, his body nearly shooting off sparks from his agitation. "How stupid could you have been? They could've given you something lethal."

"Maybe I *was* reckless, but screw you for judging me. You don't understand. I had to do it. He's a kid, and now he's *my* kid."

He leaned in closer, a palm on the tree near my head. "You think I don't get it? That I haven't lost people I was responsible for?"

"Then why can't you understand what I have to do?"

He looked away, and I dropped my gaze to the ground. We stood like that for a few minutes, as if the emotional charge between us was so strong that neither of us could handle it any longer.

"Isn't your life worth something too?" he asked softly a few minutes later.

"It's…"

"Different? You don't matter?" His tone was soft but his hands were fisted.

I shook my head, unable to explain the drive to keep Charlie safe and okay. I didn't know what had happened, but he was mine now, and that was all that seemed to matter.

He stood back, giving me more space, and I immediately missed his nearness, even though we hadn't been touching. He didn't walk away, though.

"Back or shoulder. Those are your only two choices," he said, echoing my choices when we'd first traveled here.

"Back." I spun my finger, telling him to turn around.

It was only an hour and a half on foot before we came to a cabin that looked like it could've been part of the settlement we were living in. The roof had seen better days, and part of the small porch appeared to be rotting away.

"We're here," Duncan said.

"You want to stay here?" I looked at him and then back at the teensy cabin. What was the situation with his trying to find the least desirable places to sleep? But considering why we were here, I shut up.

"This is my setup." He offered the explanation of where we were without really explaining anything.

The interior wasn't anything like I'd expected, as if the outside was intentionally dilapidated to mislead people. It had a bed, a couple of chairs with a table, a wood stove. There was even a bathroom.

He carried me over to the bed, and I sank into it like I weighed a thousand pounds.

Chapter Twenty-Six

I WOKE up hours later by myself, barely remembering getting here. I definitely didn't recall falling asleep. There was an oil lamp burning on the table alongside a pile of protein bars. I grabbed one, trying to remember when I'd eaten last.

I poked around the place, finding a pitcher of water and some glasses. The door to the cabin opened and Duncan walked in, naked and wet.

Instead of turning away, I found myself staring, my heart racing. Every amazing inch of him glistened as he walked closer to me. His gaze shot to mine and locked in, and I stopped breathing altogether.

He stopped in front of me, curving his hand around my head, tangling his fingers in my hair at the base of my skull, and his lips moved over mine. Every nerve ending I had immediately lit up like there were fireworks shooting off inside me. His lips were just feathering over mine, testing, tasting, teasing.

I'd been kissed many times, but nothing had ever undone me like the feel of his mouth on mine.

Duncan's satellite phone rang where it sat on the table, saving me from myself. I hadn't even realized he'd brought it with him.

The noise seemed to jolt us both back into reality. He took a step back, a wrinkle forming on his forehead, as if he wasn't sure how that had happened either.

He walked over and looked at the phone.

"Just Groza," he said. "I'll deal with her later."

He walked to the other side of the room, pulling out clothes from a chest. He was throwing on pants when he said, "I don't have any women's things, but I can give you a shirt and socks."

He kissed me and then went about dressing, like nothing had happened?

I took a couple of steps toward him and then stopped, afraid to get close just in case.

"What was that? Why did you do that?" I pointed to the spot of the crime, like there'd be a taped outline where we had stood.

He turned back toward me. "Sorry. I didn't mean to," he said, as if that were the end of it.

"Just so you know, that was not a good idea. I don't know why you'd want to anyway. You're pissed off at me most of the time, so why would you do that?" I put my hands on my hips. Then I crossed them in front of my chest, which brought my hard nipples to my attention. Great. No way had his eagle eyes missed that.

"Do you think people have to be in love to fuck?" His raised brow clearly established his thoughts on the matter.

It was a ridiculous statement and we both knew it. As soon as I started liking him for a second, he said or did something that reminded me that, nope, I hated him.

He was right, though. I didn't want to know why he did it. I wanted to know why I felt the way I had when he did do it. It made no sense at all. What I wanted was someone to tell me why it had felt like I was going to forget the entire world as soon as he touched me. Why had my insides burned like he'd given me more than a simple kiss? Why, of all people, did *he* have to make me feel like I was going to be incinerated as soon as we got close?

The phone rang again, and his brow furrowed.

"It's Buddie. I have to take this." He put the phone to his ear. "What's up?"

His eyes closed for a second as he leaned his head back, listening.

"And?" He let out a sigh, running a hand through his hair. He walked a few paces across the room and leaned his forearm across the top of the window as he continued to listen.

"Okay. It is what it is." He dropped the phone on the nearby chair.

"Is Charlie okay? What is it?" I said.

When he turned back toward me, there was an edge to him. The worry in his eyes was as clear to see as a stormy day.

"Charlie's fine," he said.

"Then what happened?" I sat back on bed, feeling some of the tension ease.

"Groza went into a rage over the matto incident and hit the clinic at sunset."

Hit. Knowing Groza, that probably meant razed it. There would be no going there for anything anymore.

"Is everyone okay?" I asked.

"She *hit* the clinic. Groza doesn't believe in leaving people behind who can come back and exact revenge."

"What about the people she sent?"

"None of our people died."

It looked as if there was more to come. There was one thing he wouldn't want to tell me. And it was the one thing I was afraid to ask.

"They didn't get insulin, did they?" I felt like I was asking a doctor if the prognosis was terminal, because it might be if I didn't get a supply going for Charlie.

"They got some, but Buddie said they weren't any good. I had a talk with him the other day. He knew what to look for. He says they're all cloudy."

I felt like the ground was falling out from under me. Every time there was a glimmer of hope, a possible solution, a day or so later it would be smashed to pieces. It was chipping away at my sanity and strength, little by little, until I sat here feeling like I was going to fall apart.

"We'll find another source," he said.

Except we wouldn't. The clinic had been one of the best possibilities because they had a generator. If insulin wasn't kept at a constant chilled temperature, it would go bad. In a world where there was no longer a working grid, all the supplies were going bad.

"Piper, we'll figure something out," he said, kneeling in front of me.

I nodded. I wasn't holding it together enough to have a conversation. The fact that I wasn't a blubbering mess was a miracle.

"They probably gave me the last of whatever was still good so I'd let them stick me with that tainted needle. I was scammed." I was so worried about being the bad person that I'd been duped.

"We'll find another source." Duncan did a good job of projecting conviction when we both knew it was a long shot.

The supply was diminishing. He had no idea where to get more. He was doing what people did when times were bad—feeding me bullshit so I wouldn't crack.

"What about back in New York? Is there any more there? I'll go back and get it myself. I don't need you to come. I can go." If they'd watch Charlie, I'd get back there. I could do it.

"I had Buddie pack all we had when we left. There was no more."

"Your people don't get diabetes, right?" How many werewolf movies had I seen? If Charlie was one of them, this wouldn't be an issue.

"No."

He had to know where my mind was going, but he didn't expand or elaborate. But I couldn't leave any stone unturned.

"Could you... Is there a way..."

"We're born this way. There have been some who have tried, but most of them die attempting it. If I thought it was a possibility, I would've offered."

"How long do I need to stay here before it's safe for the shifters to be around me? I have to get back. I can't sit here. I have to go do something."

"It's already fading. We should be able to leave by first light tomorrow."

Chapter Twenty-Seven

THE SHIFT in the energy as we walked back into the pack was palpable. When they used to stare at me before, it was a mixture of dislike and hesitancy. That had changed dramatically since my last offense of unwittingly carrying something that could've taken them out. I still had no idea what the people in the clinic had meant to do, or if it had been intentional, but this pack looked at me as if I'd been in on it. Now they gave me hard looks, like they were debating killing me. I had a feeling Duncan was the only thing holding them back.

I no longer cared. The only thing that mattered was getting more insulin for Charlie.

The second I was back in the cottage, I went through the stash of insulin, *again*. It was getting to be all I could think of, with every other thought crowded out. All the vials were getting cloudy. I'd known it was going to happen because they were all the same kind, probably similar age, and kept in the same conditions. It didn't mean they wouldn't work at all, but it was like sitting on a ticking time bomb. Every day they'd work a little less.

Charlie needed new insulin and I had no idea where to start. This wasn't like the city, with twenty pharmacies within an hour's bike ride. Even if I did find a pharmacy, odds were their supplies might be going bad as well.

Duncan walked into the kitchen, stopping beside me. "Rastin, Trevor, and Birdie are out looking now."

"I need to go, too."

"They can cover ground faster without you," Duncan said.

I looked up at him. "I can't sit here and do nothing."

"You'll slow them down if you go with them."

After I'd traveled with them, there was no denying it. They'd cover at least twice as much area without me.

"Then you and Buddie should go with them. The more people looking, the better." I wanted to push him out the door and get him moving. We didn't have time to sit here and debate any of this.

"I'm not leaving you here alone right now. Not after the way we left—and what I was feeling when we walked back in."

He was giving me a look as if I should know better. I did. What he was missing was that I didn't care. I wasn't letting Charlie die. That was the beginning and end of it.

"I'm not afraid. You're more useful out there." I pointed to the door, wishing I could force him to go look.

He put his hands on the counter, caging me in with an arm on either side. "I'm *not* leaving. I don't like the feeling I'm getting around here. I think there's going to be a lot of anger after this, and this isn't my pack. I can't control them. You need to be careful."

He was leaning close enough that a few inches less and we'd be touching.

"Duncan," Buddie called from the door.

Duncan straightened away from me but not before giving me a warning glance. "Don't forget what I said. No one will do anything to you where there are witnesses because they know they'll be dealing with me. Don't disappear on your own."

I nodded, just to placate him, and watched him hesitantly turn to leave with Buddie. I didn't have the energy to fight over my safety when Charlie's life was the one in peril.

I needed someone with knowledge of the area, who was also willing to give me that information. Since most of the people here wanted nothing to do with me, that left only one person: Catarina.

I made my way toward her office, ignoring the looks and moving out of the way when someone purposely seemed to step in front of me.

I hovered on Catarina's stoop, in plain sight of where she was sitting as I rapped on the open door.

She put down her pencil and waved. "Come just inside the door, no farther. I want to make sure I don't catch a whiff of something off."

I did as she asked, afraid to go even one more step than instructed. Her nostrils flared and her chest rose. "Okay, you smell normal," she said, waving me in.

I walked another few steps but still hesitated. "I'm really sorry about what happened."

"No harm done. I didn't get sick." She glanced at the chair and then back to me. "Are you going to sit?"

"That's awfully close. You're sure?" I didn't want to take out one of the only people who still didn't seem to hate me.

"I said it was okay."

I took the seat before she got irritated and put me on some crap duty, literally.

"I heard about the insulin," she said.

I nodded, trying to formulate a coherent string of words when the thought of Charlie running out made my engine seize up.

"Duncan will figure out something," she said, leaning closer and patting my hand. From Catarina, that hand pat was the equivalent of a bear hug.

"Yeah. About that. Would you happen to have any idea of places around here that might have some insulin?"

She leaned back and sighed. "Duncan already asked as well. I can't think of anything off the top of my head, but I'm racking my brain to come up with some possibilities."

"Thanks. I appreciate anything you can think of."

She nodded the way people do when they know they aren't going to really be able to help.

"So, I wasn't going to give you anything today because, well, mostly I figured you might be a mess and useless. But there's been a request from Jaysa. She wants to see you."

"Jaysa? All-in-black Jaysa?" I stopped short of calling her creepy Jaysa.

Catarina nodded, and there was definitely a little more sympathy in her gaze.

"Any idea why?" I twisted my hands together. Jaysa had freaked me out *before* I'd almost gotten her entire pack sick. That had to be why she wanted to see me. Was someone in the pack using her to lure me over and kill me? Did they think I wouldn't be scared of the older lady, so I'd walk into that deathtrap like a trusting idiot?

"I want to know, too. She sent a kid over with a note requesting you, but the kid didn't know either. No one usually questions Jaysa. We all give her plenty of space."

I wasn't going to run to Duncan after I'd told him I wasn't scared of anything. I needed to get him out there searching for insulin. Making him hold my hand to go talk to Jaysa wasn't going to encourage that. I wasn't hiding, either. That was for sure. Plus, they called her a guide. Maybe, just maybe, she'd have some sort of magic voodoo thing that might help? I wasn't above trying anything.

"Well, I guess I don't want to leave her waiting." I stood up but needed another moment before I could get my legs to move toward the door.

"Better to rip the bandage off." Catarina gave me a thumbs-up.

"See you tomorrow. Hopefully," I said.

She nodded but grimaced, and notably didn't say anything to reassure me that I was worrying over nothing. That wasn't confidence inspiring.

I stepped out of Catarina's building and hesitated on the porch, catching more glares. Young, old, male, female, they all hated me. I lifted my chin another inch and walked to Jaysa's.

I knocked on her door.

"Come in," she called.

Her place was dark for midday, with draperies on the window. Jaysa kept the fireplace barely burning, and there was not a candle in sight. Once I shut the door, it could've been midnight. Her form was barely visible on the chair in the corner.

"You wanted to see me?" I certainly hadn't wanted to see her. No part of me had walked over here thinking *yippee*. Where some of the shifters could destroy me physically, there was something else about her, an energy in the air around her, hinting at things unknown. Of all the shifters in this place, she freaked me out the worst.

Even the other shifters seemed to avoid her. If they were

scared, what the hell was I going to do? The way she looked at me, like she was taking me apart, didn't help matters.

"Sit."

I was pretty sure she wasn't referring to one of the chairs at the table, but the one right next to her.

I forced myself to cross the room, wondering what it was about her that set my nerves on edge. I'd survived Death Day, discovered monsters, now lived surrounded by those monsters, and yet this old woman made me want to run screaming from the room while she did nothing but exist.

"Do you know how old I am?"

The question made me feel like an earthworm plucked up and thrown on hot pavement. It wasn't like I could tell her that she didn't look a day over forty. Her lines had lines. Her eyes were glazed over with a layer of white so thick that I didn't know how she could see. She probably hadn't stood up straight in a good twenty years.

"Eighty? Ninety?" Even that was being generous. Widow Herbert had been in her nineties and looked like a spring chicken compared to this woman.

"I'm one thousand, four hundred, and twenty-two years old. Our kind live longer, although not as long as me."

Whoa. I might've gasped when she said it. It was a little tough to act like I'd been there, done that, and seen it all when I was dealing with someone who had truly been there and seen it all.

What was the normal range? How old were the guys? I'd thought maybe they had a decade on me, not a century.

She didn't say anything else as she sat there watching *me*.

She kept watching me for a few minutes until she finally said, "Let me see your hand."

I almost didn't give it to her. As it was, I jumped at the feel of her grasp. It wasn't a normal flesh-on-flesh feeling. It felt like touching something with a low voltage running through them. There wasn't a shifter I'd touched yet that felt like her.

"Are you…" I didn't finish. Asking her why she made me feel like I was sucking on the end of a battery wasn't smart. I needed to let her say what she wanted and get it out of her system. I had enough trouble coming for me without looking for it.

"As I said, I'm not like everyone else here." She nailed me with a gaze that felt like it was digging around in my head.

She sat there holding my hand for another few seconds, and then released me.

"Duncan puts his people first," she said. "Always has. He wouldn't ever do something he thinks would hurt the pack."

Was that some sort of warning? A message to me?

"I wouldn't ask him to." Someone was clearly getting in her ear. Yes, I'd wanted help finding insulin, had perhaps screwed up at the clinic, but everyone was fine. I couldn't think of another instance of harm she could lay at my doorstep.

She tilted her head one way then the other.

"While I'm here, do you know of anything that would help someone that has a problem like diabetes?" Even as I asked, I felt like an idiot. That didn't stop me from waiting for her answer.

"For that sickly cub of yours?" she said.

Something about that term got my back up. I got to my feet. "He's fine. He just needs medication. Can you help or no?"

"No one can help a *human* with that."

I couldn't believe I'd wasted time coming here and listening to this crackpot. She clearly hated humans too. "You said you wanted to speak to me. Is there anything else? I have other things I need to do."

"I needed to take your measure, and I have. You can go," she said.

Yeah, she hated me, and I didn't care. She could get in line.

I made my way to the school, looking around for Charlie. The kids were outside playing. I slowed, trying to hide behind some bushes. He and a few other boys were under a big oak tree with a tire swing. Two boys were in the tire, and Charlie and another boy were on top, swinging back and forth.

"Captain, I see a storm blowing in!" Charlie yelled from the top of the tire as a boy below pretended to have binoculars. I backed away, not wanting to interrupt his fun. The adults might hate me, but it hadn't bled down to Charlie.

Buddie spotted me and walked over. Although I wasn't sure if it was a coincidence he'd seen me or if Duncan had sent him to keep tabs.

"He's doing well," he said, coming to stand beside me and watch them. "The kids here all like him. They've accepted him."

"For now, while they're all similar. It won't be like that forever." I was living proof.

"Hopefully we'll have something else worked out by then," Buddie said, like Duncan's pack would end up being any better. No, this was a stopgap situation only. I might be distracted enough with other pressing problems to push it out of my day-to-day thoughts, but the reality would always be there. We'd never be accepted in the pack.

Chapter Twenty-Eight

I'D NEVER BEEN one to bounce out of bed at first light, bright-eyed and bushy-tailed. I also didn't typically feel like I couldn't unbend my joints. Everything in my body was stiff. Was it the flu? I didn't feel feverish. No chills, no lethargy, only this strange feeling of exhaustion and my joints not working. Or was it my muscles that were weak and refused to cooperate? I stretched out my fingers, and my hand shook from the exertion.

"Why do you look weird?" Charlie asked, staring at me from the bedroom door.

I dropped my hands to the bed, gripping the blanket. His world had been thrown upside down, but as long as I seemed normal, he appeared to accept things a little easier. If I was smiling, he seemed to believe the world was okay. As soon as I was a little off, he froze up like it was truly the end of the world.

"Hey, you're not going to be making friends with girls if you go around telling them they look weird." I gave him the best teasing grin I could muster. "I woke up later than usual because I was facing away from the window, so the sun didn't tell me it was time to rise."

His little brain seemed to contemplate this story, and then he giggled. "I don't want to make friends with girls. I'm a boy!" His smile stayed, but he still sounded a tiny bit worried as he asked, "You're getting up now, though, right?"

He was probably thinking of our father. He couldn't quite put the whole picture together at five, but he knew how wrong that situation had been.

"Of course I am. I'm certainly not going to stay in bed all day. That would be silly, since I'm not sick." I waited, not completely confident I'd be able to pass his five-year-old scrutiny when I attempted to rise.

"Okay," he said, finally giving his nod of approval. But he didn't leave.

"Hey, is Duncan up?" I needed to get this kid moving. I didn't want to make a liar out of myself in front of him.

"Yes. He's making us breakfast." He grinned. "Pancakes!"

"Okay, well, you better get down there and make sure he doesn't eat them all."

"He wouldn't do that." Charlie giggled.

"I don't know. I don't think we should risk it."

That got him moving down the stairs. "Duncan, don't eat them all!"

I pushed my body upward. Even bending at the waist seemed hard, but I pushed forward, getting to my feet. I stretched out my arms several times, my hands trembling. I shook them out, trying to get rid of it. The shaking in my hands was now spreading to my legs. Was I dying? How would I even know? Not like I could find a doctor to check me out, run a couple tests, check my blood work.

What if Jaysa had cursed me? There wasn't a doctor alive that would be able to diagnose that kind of sickness.

At least I was out of bed. I bent forward then straightened. Then I did it again, and then another ten times, feeling like it was getting a little better with each bend. I started working on my legs next.

"Pancakes are getting cold!" Charlie yelled from below.

"I'll be there in a few minutes. I'm trying to decide what to wear."

I grabbed the first pair of jeans I laid eyes on, figuring I'd change later if needed. I just had to get through this morning until he got off to school.

Duncan was at the base of the stairs when I finally made my way down.

His gaze traveled from my hair down to my t-shirt, where I was suddenly very aware that I hadn't put on a bra. The heat in his eyes seemed to ignite an equal warmth in me. I crossed my arms, trying to hide the telltale signs.

"I left some pancakes on the table. I'm going to walk him over to school."

"Thanks."

"Bye, Piper." Charlie waved at me and then latched on to Duncan like he was his dad. How the hell was I ever going to take him out of here? Duncan might not feel the loss, but Charlie would be devastated.

Buddie walked in a few minutes later. "Where's Duncan?"

"He's walking Charlie to school. Want some pancakes?" I motioned to the heap in the center of the table. I wasn't sure how much Duncan thought I could eat, but that mountain of goodness wasn't in the realm of reality.

Buddie looked them over, hesitating.

"Duncan made them. They're edible." I said.

225

"Oh, yeah, that wasn't it. I wanted to make sure you had enough." He grabbed a plate.

Bull. Word was obviously getting out.

For someone supposedly worried about taking too much, he wiped out three-quarters of the stack.

"You know what I miss? Chocolate chips. I loved chocolate chips with my pancakes," he said.

"I'd kill for blueberries right now. I don't even like blueberries."

"That's an easy one. There's a whole pile set aside for Jaysa."

"Have you lost your mind? There's no way I'm taking her berries. I'm lucky she hasn't killed me already." She might've already tried, considering the way I was feeling. What if I had a wasting disease?

"Didn't you hear? That's not a problem anymore. She passed last night." He took another big bite of pancakes, the news apparently not denting his appetite.

"She's dead?" Well, at least she wouldn't be around to kill me. Unless she'd already done something.

He leaned forward. "Strangest part about it is she told people she was going to die that night. I mean, our guides have an *idea* when they're going to pass, but not usually the exact moment."

"She told people she was going to die?" I asked, not believing it for a second. It wasn't like I could double-check their story. Some people had a flair for drama when they told a story and weren't averse to exaggerating here and there.

"Look, I wouldn't have believed it either, but this guy told me last night *before* she died." He finished up the last pancake on his plate and then looked at the rest of the stack in the center. "You mind?"

I pushed the plate toward him. "Maybe she wasn't feeling well and knew somehow?"

"She didn't look any worse for wear. You know, worse than normal." He drowned the last of the pancakes in so much syrup that there wasn't a speck of plate left to be seen.

"What did she actually do for the pack? She was supposed to be some sort of spiritual guide or something, right?"

"She kept the packs in balance, not just this one but the entire East Coast." He stopped eating and added, "It's really freaking people out that she's gone, me included. Most guides hand off their magic before they die, but she didn't. It might sound like weird hocus-pocus, but there's a lot of things out there we don't fully understand."

"Yeah, I feel like I've gotten a crash course in that." She'd probably used up the last of the magic she had to kill me.

Chapter Twenty-Nine

I SLUMPED down into the chair at Catarina's.

She looked up from her desk and took a deep breath, as if assuring herself whatever was wrong with me wasn't anything catching. "Why do you look so lousy?"

"I don't know, but I'm fine." Nothing was fine. It was another day, and still no word on insulin. Every morning I looked at the vials, trying to determine if they were cloudier. I'd stare until I thought I was seeing things.

And it had been another morning where I needed half an hour to stretch out the stiffness. I was so tired it felt like I had a foot in the grave.

Screaming caught my attention, and I glanced toward the open door. In the distance, a woman and a man were both standing on the porch of Jaysa's cabin, drawing a crowd.

"I'd steer clear of that area," Catarina said. "Everyone is trying to claim Jaysa's cabin, and all that it entails."

The woman on the porch cocked her arm back and then cracked the guy in the jaw. Before things could escalate, some of the bystanders rushed in between them.

"Wow, they *really* want that cabin."

"Like I said, it's what comes with it. By claiming the cabin, they're saying they're Jaysa's replacement."

"Are they?" I was on my feet, over by the window, watching them fight. Catarina hadn't bothered to look up from her desk.

"No one knows yet. Our guides don't usually just die, or I don't think they do. They're supposed to pass on what they are to someone else in one of the packs in the area and make it known. She didn't do that."

"Has that ever happened before?"

"Who knows? She's lived so long that no one was around last time it happened, but it's causing a lot of upheaval. Yesterday those two almost simultaneously started saying they felt her powers growing in them. Knowing them, it's more likely to be indigestion. The only thing I do know for sure is that it'll be obvious. We'll all be able to sense it. Even you, with your limited senses, knew Jaysa was different."

She was right about that. There'd been something different about that woman that made your hair stand on end.

"Have you thought about the insulin issue? Any ideas?" I asked, dragging my attention away from Jaysa's cabin.

"Yeah, I told Duncan about a possibility this morning," she said.

"When was that?" It was still morning. I got up, ate, dropped Charlie off at school, and came right here. It couldn't have been past nine.

"A little before dawn? By the time you come in, I'm ready for my break. Our race is crepuscular. We're most awake and active around dawn and dusk. We also don't need as much sleep as humans. Most of us can get by on two or three hours."

It was hard not to start getting an inferiority complex

around here. It had probably been another way I'd slowed the guys down when we were traveling, and why Duncan had said I'd only hold them back in the search for insulin.

It was hard not to feel like a slacker, but I'd contemplate that later. Right now I had to go find Duncan and see if there was any word on insulin. He'd been missing this morning, maybe because of this?

"Would you mind if I go take care of something else today?" I was already edging back toward the door.

"Figured you'd want to go check in with Duncan. I think I saw him by the barn." She waved a hand and went back to whatever she'd been working on.

"Thanks, Catarina."

"Not an issue," she said.

It was becoming clear that this job was more about keeping up appearances than actually contributing, in her estimation. That was another issue I'd worry about tomorrow.

I made my way across the community and to the barn. Duncan wasn't anywhere outside.

"Duncan?" I called from the opening of the barn. I went a bit farther in.

"Duncan isn't here. Can I be of help?"

I spun, finding a man I'd seen around before standing in the opening. Mannie wasn't a bad-looking guy, but something about his stare had always struck me as meaner than most. Another two men appeared beside him, one with a half a bottle of booze in his hand.

"I'm fine. I thought I was supposed to meet Duncan here, but he must've meant at the cottage." I took a couple wary steps toward the door, hoping one of them would shift out of my way. They didn't.

Mannie's eyes roved up and down my body. It was unfortunate how instead of rising to be a hero in times like these, some people embraced Death Day as the starting flag on a race to the bottom. Me having almost wiped out his pack probably didn't help.

"Duncan sure seems to have taken a liking to you. Wonder what all the fuss is about?" Mannie took a step closer.

"I need to get going. He gets worried when I'm late." The longer I lingered, the longer they'd all have to decide their bad ideas were good. I tried to sidestep around Mannie.

"I think you should hang out with us for a little while," he said, snaking an arm around my waist.

"You're asking for trouble." I tried to sound as firm as I could, as if I had some authority.

His friends snickered.

"I'm not sure you realize this yet, but you're a human," Mannie said. "Other than Duncan, no one here gives a shit about what I do to you. In fact, they might be happy if something were to happen to you." He leaned in, making a show of smelling my neck.

There were three of them, not that it mattered. One was already too much for me to handle, especially knowing how they could shift. If I fought, they might kill me. If they took this farther, it would be easier for them to off me afterward. They might look stupid, but they were smart enough to know to get rid of my body after they were done with me. Leaving any kind of evidence would cause an issue with Duncan and the guys. What would happen to Charlie? Who would take care of him? Would Buddie honor his promise to take care of my brother?

Mannie held me to his chest with one arm and grabbed my hair with the other hand. He held my head steady as I tried to jerk it out of his grasp. He kissed me with a grinding pressure that had nothing to do with pleasure and everything to do with causing as much pain as possible. I gagged on the alcohol and tobacco taste of him.

"Hey," one of the friends said, ripping me out of Mannie's grasp and leaving a chunk of my hair twisted around his fist. "Don't be a hog."

He'd balanced his liquor bottle on the edge of the door beside him. I moved in closer to him, trying to get within reach of the bottle.

"She likes me," the friend said. I wrapped an arm around his neck, leaning in and grabbing the bottle. I leaned back and swung it at his head. The bottle broke on his skull and the jagged glass slashed his face.

He let out a scream, letting go of me as his hands went to his face. I turned and plowed right into another chest—but this one was Duncan's.

"What's going on here?" he growled.

"We didn't do anything. She came to us," Mannie said, looking behind him as if checking to see if there was another exit out of the barn, with the same desperation I had moments ago.

"Nothing happened," I said, pulling away from Duncan and taking a few steps away from the scene of the crime.

He looked at me. "Nothing?"

"Yes. Nothing." This situation was enough of a mess. There were three of them, and that was just here in the barn. As far as the community, there were hundreds who would willingly gang up against a handful of men from a different pack. Groza certainly wouldn't step up.

"See? Nothing happened," Mannie said, smirking.

I started walking in the opposite direction, hoping I'd lure Duncan away with me.

"If you touch her again, you're dead. You walk too close to her on the street and accidentally graze her, you're dead. Do you understand me?" Duncan said.

"She's a fucking worthless human," Mannie replied.

"You might also lose a tongue if you don't shut up," Duncan said.

That was the last thing I could hear as I kept walking, hoping my tactic would work.

I sensed Duncan nearing a few minutes later.

"Why are you protecting them?" he asked.

"It's fine. Nothing really happened, and as you can see, they're worse off than me." I kept heading back to the cottage, not looking back. This was going to be life here now.

"You don't look fine."

If I didn't, it had more to do with the stress of getting insulin than those fools. That was probably why I felt like I had the flu. It was tension building up in me, making me feel weak. "I've got bigger worries than a few idiots. Catarina told me she gave you a lead on insulin?"

"I gave Birdie the information. No luck yet. I needed to talk to you about a few other things as well," he said, opening the door to the cottage.

I walked into the kitchen, grabbing a glass of water to wipe away the foul taste of Mannie. I would've spit it back out if that wouldn't tip off Duncan on how unsettled I really was.

"I went and checked out a human community nearby. I made some connections and agreements there. It would be a place you and Charlie could go that might be safer." He rested his hands on the back of a chair, looking like he might split the wood.

"Don't you think you should've asked me first? Maybe brought me along so I could see if it was somewhere I wanted to go?" I had a love-hate relationship with Duncan's constant interference in my life. As soon as I was grateful for one thing, he felt high-handed somewhere else. It was clear that pack life worked differently than what I was used to, and it might be a good thing I was eventually leaving—maybe sooner than later, if he had anything to do with it.

There was no denying that this situation was becoming bad, but it hadn't bled over to Charlie yet. This was not the time to uproot him. The added stress would make his adrenaline spike and chew up insulin, not to mention the heartache. Plus, when I did get the boot, it would at least be to a destination of my choosing.

"This place is becoming unsafe. You won't have to leave forever. Once I get the pack set up somewhere new, I'll come for you."

"I can figure out a place on my own when the time comes, but I can't leave yet. It's bad for Charlie," I said.

"It's worse for you to stay. I'm trying to help you." He took a step closer.

"Well, you aren't making it easier to leave. He looks at you like you're a god. Now he has to lose another person? Yeah, thanks for the help." I shook my head and turned to walk away.

"Am I supposed to be mean to the kid so it would be easier for you?" he asked, blocking the kitchen door.

"Maybe you should've kept some distance if you wanted us gone?" And maybe not just with Charlie, either. He was kissing me and defending me one minute and then kicking us to the curb the next. I wasn't a kid, and it was giving *me* whiplash.

"What? You think I *want* you two to leave? That I want to constantly worry about you?"

"Maybe you should make up your mind on whether you hate me or want me. You don't even like me most days, and then others you're kissing me, and then you tell me how I have to leave." I felt like a volcano erupting and spewing every thought in my head, like I was incapable of holding it back anymore.

His jaw twitched, as if he hated the reminder.

"Oh, is that the problem? You don't like the fact that you want to sleep with me?" He was so close to me now that his toes were almost grazing mine.

He wouldn't answer, but he didn't have to. It was driving him crazy to want me, a human. Guess that wasn't in his game plan.

"I'm sorry I've been such a strain to have to think about, but you can relax. I'll be leaving soon enough." I shoved him with everything I had, but he didn't move.

"Don't. Touch. Me," he said.

"Or what?"

It was like our energy was ricocheting off each other, building until we detonated.

I shoved at his chest, then shoved again, as if I couldn't stop touching him.

"I hate you," I said.

Heat flared in his eyes. "We both know that's a lie."

He grabbed my hips, walking me back the last couple feet to the wall and pinning me there. His leg found its way in between mine, and my breathing roughened at the contact.

I planted my hands on his pecs, finding it hard to ignore how chiseled his chest felt under my palms. I shifted slightly, and the pressure of his leg between mine made it hard to stand still.

He pulled me into him.

"You're playing a dangerous game." He moved his hand from the wall beside me to trail it along my neck, down my sternum, not touching anything of consequence and yet making me yearn more for contact than I'd ever craved from a human.

"I do hate you. You're the last person I'd ever sleep with." My breathless declaration couldn't even convince me.

"No interest at all?" He rocked his hips against mine, just the smallest movement, the slightest pressure, and I let out a moan.

"None. I'd rather forsake men for life than to be with you." Forget breathless—I was panting, and no number of lies were going to hide my arousal.

He reached down, wrapping a hand around my thigh and hoisting me farther up the wall until he fit between my legs more snugly, more intimately. I could feel his huge cock pressing right where I craved him most.

He shifted again, causing that glorious friction. I gripped his shoulders, and a hoarse groan escaped my lips.

"Tell me you hate me again," he said in a low growl.

"I…" He rocked against me again, and I couldn't speak. I was going to come, fully clothed, simply because he was pressing against me, and not even the humiliation of that made me want to push him away.

He wrapped his hands under my other thigh, pulling my legs around him. Duncan's mouth covered mine as his hips jerked against me. His kiss covered my moan as I came close to exploding.

The front door slammed open.

"Duncan! Piper!" Buddie yelled.

"Not now," Duncan said.

"It's Charlie."

Chapter Thirty

BUDDIE STOOD BY THE DOOR, an unconscious Charlie in his arms.

I let out a cry that didn't sound human as I rushed to them. "What happened?"

He shook his head, looking at Charlie's limp body. "The teacher said he was running around with the kids outside and started acting weird. Then he dropped to the ground as I happened to be passing by."

"Lay him down." I grabbed some insulin, filled a needle, and ran back to him.

I put the shot into Charlie's stomach, fearing it wouldn't make a difference. The insulin was going bad. Was it working at all? I'd given him more than I should've, hoping the quantity would compensate for the poor quality.

"Will that fix him?" Buddie asked.

Duncan was eerily quiet as he held Charlie's tiny wrist in his hand.

"I don't know, but it's all I have." We didn't move, all staring at his lifeless form, hoping he'd stir.

A few more minutes went by with no change. "I need more insulin."

Duncan was already handing me another vial before I could go get it. I refilled the needle and shot Charlie up again. If it was going to work, there would be a sign fairly quickly. But as we all waited, watching him, there wasn't a flicker of movement.

I looked up at Duncan. "You have to try to turn him."

"It's a high rate of death. It's safer to give him more insulin and wait a little while longer," he said.

"Except it's not working!" I got to my feet, grabbing his shirt and trying to drag him over. "Just try! He's going to die!"

"Give me a few minutes," he said, pulling out of my grasp and heading toward the door.

"Where are you going?" I yelled.

He took off.

"Can you do it?" I asked Buddie.

He shook his head. "The few transitions that have worked were only with alphas. It would be a death sentence."

The minutes ticked by, and Charlie wasn't waking up. I'd carried him upstairs to his bed, trying to make him comfortable, covering him with his blanket and hugging him to keep him warm, but nothing mattered. He was in a coma.

If I'd stayed in the city, I might've been able to get him more insulin. There might've been other options, but I'd dragged him here, and now he was going to die. I hadn't been able to keep my mother alive, I'd killed Widow Herbert by bringing her with me, and now Charlie might die.

I cradled him in my arms, praying that he could feel me, take my strength into his small body. I prayed to God to take my life and give it to Charlie.

It didn't matter what I did, because he wasn't waking.

There were sounds below, and then Buddie was in the door. "Duncan is back with Groza. She wants to talk to you."

"I don't care. If that pisses her off, she can come back in a couple of days and kill me at that point." By then Charlie would be dead, and I'd be grateful if she finished me off.

"Piper, I think you want to talk to her. I'll stay with Charlie."

"Does she have insulin? Because that is the only way I'll care."

"No, but she's got another solution." He took a tentative step toward the bed, as if fearing I'd start swinging at him if he forced me to leave Charlie.

"Really?"

"Yes."

I scrambled out of the bed, only slowing to make sure Buddie went and sat with Charlie. "Hold his hand. I want him to know he's not alone."

Buddie nodded, doing as I asked, even climbing into bed with Charlie.

I raced downstairs, knowing every minute counted.

Duncan and Groza were standing on the porch, looking like they were facing off before a cage match.

"Can you fix him?" I asked Groza, stepping in between them.

"I might be able to, but it's not that simple. We need to talk."

"I'll be waiting inside," Duncan said, looking as if he'd just been given a death sentence himself.

His expression didn't infuse me with any hope.

"Well?" I asked, having no patience to waste time on Groza if she couldn't help.

"There have been certain people, and ways, that have

turned children. It can be done more successfully than adults, and the younger the better. There are certain techniques I know of that put the survival rate at over fifty percent for a cub his age, but they'll require Duncan *and* myself. He can't do it alone, and I have a price."

"What's your price?" A fifty percent survival rate didn't sound wonderful unless you were staring down at zero, like I was. Now? A fifty-fifty chance of him living was a miracle.

She crossed her arms, glaring at me. "If the transition is successful, you can't take him from the pack. He'll need shifters to learn from, for numbers, for protection. He'll be one of our kind, and I won't let you put him in jeopardy."

"Fine." This wasn't the life I'd imagined for him, but we'd work through it because he'd be alive.

"But *you* have to leave. That's my price."

She'd wanted to get rid of me from the moment I set foot in this place, and now she had her opportunity.

I hated this woman, more every day and never as much as right now. But I could hear the truth when she said it. He'd need these people, and my days were limited here as it was. The price of Charlie's survival would be my broken heart, but it would hurt a thousand times worse if he died. There was no question of agreeing. Duncan would be breaking off from Gorza's pack one day. He would have his own pack here soon, and they would be looking for a new place to settle. I'd be able to be with Charlie when that happened. This wouldn't be forever.

Plus, there wasn't a choice. It had to happen, and I had nothing to negotiate with. I accepted her terms or Charlie died.

"I agree. Save him."

"You sure you want to make that deal? Because I'll be expecting you to leave as soon as we know he's going to make it. Once a promise is given, you will be leaving one way or another."

"Yes. Save him and I'll give you whatever you want. Just do it." I pointed at the door. We didn't have time to rehash this. I'd agreed. I'd agree another thousand times if that was what it took.

She walked into the cottage, turning to Duncan. "Get prepared. You'll need to shift."

"Buddie, bring Charlie down," Duncan yelled.

Buddie came down a minute later, with Charlie looking so tiny and frail in his arms.

"Put him on the couch," Groza said. She turned to Duncan. "Do you need to take some precautions?" She nodded in my direction.

He looked at Buddie. "You need to take her out of here for a bit."

Groza looked at Duncan as if he'd just landed a punch to her gut. Then she turned to me, as if *I'd* told him to punch her.

"I can't stay?"

"No," Duncan said. "You need to leave, and now. We don't have a lot of time. His vitals aren't good."

"I'll take care of her." Buddie turned to me and nodded toward the door.

I ran to Charlie first, hugging him and saying another prayer, hoping it wasn't the last time I saw him alive.

I walked out with Buddie a minute later. Every time I stopped walking, he urged me along.

"Where are we going? I don't want to be too far from him." I kept glancing over my shoulder, watching the cottage, which was almost out of view. "Why can't I wait there? Is it because I'm human or something?"

"Or something," he said.

"What do you mean?"

His lips were pressed together, as if he already regretted saying that much.

"What is it?" I said.

"It's just that things can get unpredictable during shifting, and with that kind of situation? It's better to eliminate possible problems. Nothing to be worried about."

His attempt at a reassuring me had me backtracking toward the house.

"Is there something weird with me when he shifts? Like, does he get some strange urge to kill me or eat me or something?" This was definitely something I should know before Duncan shifted with Charlie. "You better explain yourself if you want me to take one more step."

"There might be an urge, but not like that. Charlie is fine. Now can you keep walking?" Buddie's brows rose and he waved his hands to usher me along.

I didn't move. "Then what—"

"I'm not sure talking about this is the best idea." He looked at the cottage and then me.

"I don't think walking this far from the cottage while who knows what is happening to Charlie is a good idea. If you want me to keep walking, you need to tell me why I can't be there." I pointed back toward the cottage.

"Look, whatever is happening with this world is throwing all sorts of things off-kilter, including Duncan. He seems to be getting a little…" He stalled, as if trying to figure out a proper term. "Let's just say he gets *overprotective* of you at times, and we don't want him distracted while he's doing what he's doing."

"Overprotective?" I thought back to when we'd camped out on our way here and he made sure he slept closest to me.

Or how he'd gotten his hackles up when he smelled Rastin on me. "You mean like overly worried about other *men* around me?" Somehow that sounded better than saying he might be jealous, which felt absurd.

"Yes. You could put it that way." Buddie looked all around, as if afraid someone would overhear us.

"You said he's off-kilter, though. That's not going to affect what he's doing, right?"

"No, it won't. I meant because he's so protective of a human. Humans might be acceptable..." He shut up, realizing he'd said too much *again*. "Look, it's just not how things work. I mean, shifters might hook up with humans on occasion, but..."

Those words felt like a steel rod shoved down my spine.

"Humans are good for one-night stands, you mean?"

"Look, it's no different than when you were explaining to Widow Herbert that we're monsters. Interspecies hookups have difficulties. He's not going to eat Charlie, but we need to give them space. Can we leave it at that?"

I shook my head, not caring at all about any of this right now. I wanted to get back to the cottage and Charlie.

"Fine. Humans are trash. Whatever. Can we turn around yet or not?"

He looked at the setting sun, trying to gauge how much time had passed. "Give it five more minutes and then we'll walk back really slowly."

I was already about to crawl out of my skin now. "Three."

"Fine."

I waited two before I took a tiny step back toward the cottage.

Duncan was on his way out, only a pair of pants on. He

glanced in my direction, and my breathing halted—even from this distance, I caught the heat in his eyes.

He took off in a blur. I nearly ran the rest of the way. Groza walked out of the cottage as I closed the distance.

"As soon as we know Charlie is going to make it, I want you gone," she said, stopping in front of me.

I didn't say anything. She hated me; I despised her. None of that mattered right now. I rushed past her and to Charlie where he was lying on the couch.

I ran a hand over his head. He was sleeping deeply, but his chest was rising and falling normally. His skin was flushed with color, the gray pallor gone. On his arm, there were two bite marks that looked as if they were already scabbing over.

I hugged his little body, hoping for the best.

Chapter Thirty-One

CHARLIE DIDN'T OPEN his eyes until the next morning. I'd lain beside him, checking his breathing all night, waiting for him to wake. Finally, those long lashes started to flutter.

He looked up at me and smiled. "I got sick at school," he said, as if it was a small inconvenience.

"I know. But you're okay now." My voice cracked as I spoke. He was going to be okay. Really okay. There wouldn't be any more sleepless nights wondering where I'd find insulin. No more days examining the vials I had left, watching them slowly go bad. It was done. He'd be stronger than he'd ever been before.

"Why are you crying?" he asked.

"Because you're not going to need your medicine anymore, and that makes me very happy." I hugged him again, having a hard time letting him go.

"I don't?" He looked at me with huge eyes, lips parted.

"No." I wiped my face with my arm, trying to control the

flow of tears. "You're going to be a little different now, but healthier. You're going to be like the guys."

"Really?" His eyes went even bigger, like I'd told him he was getting video games back or something. "Will I be able to become a monster, too?"

"Well, maybe soon. I'm not exactly sure how it'll work, but you won't need the medicine anymore."

He shot up in bed. "Can I do it now?"

His face was scrunched up, as if he were trying to become a monster right here and now.

"I don't think so." It was hard not to laugh at his continued efforts. "You'll have to talk to the guys about it. They know more than I do. What's more important is how you feel."

"I feel good." I could tell that all he was thinking about now was turning into a monster, no matter what I said.

"I'll hang out with him if you need a minute," Buddie said from the open door.

"Buddie! When can I be a monster?" Charlie asked, completely forgetting about me and leaping out of the bed to get to him.

"Okay, but just for a couple minutes," I said—not that Charlie was listening to me. The two of them were already having a monster powwow as I left the room.

I walked downstairs into the kitchen, grabbed a glass of water, and collapsed into a chair. Every part of me, from my body to my mind, felt frayed beyond repair. I wanted to cry from relief and sob because of what was going to come next. How was I going to tell him I was leaving?

My mind raced as I tried to figure out what happened next. Repercussions bounced around in my head so fast, it felt like my skull was going to break from the ricochet.

Duncan walked in and leaned against the table where I was sitting.

"He's going to make it," he said.

He'd been gone all night, not that it bothered me. He'd helped to save Charlie, and I'd be grateful until I died.

"He wanted to know when he'd shift." I laughed softly, thinking about how hard Charlie had been concentrating on it and how excited it made him.

"He most likely won't fully transition until he hits puberty. There's time to talk him through the finer details."

"You saved him. Thank you. I appreciate that more than I can express." I dropped my chin into my palm, biting my lower lip.

He was going to grow up with them. Have a community. He was going to have a family, even if I wasn't part of that. I didn't want to leave him, but he would be okay. He'd have to be, because I didn't have a choice. I'd told him I'd never leave. I'd made a promise to him that I shouldn't have, and now I'd pay the piper.

"How do I tell him I have to leave when he's already lost so much?" I stared at Duncan, trying to hold back the hope that he'd somehow come up with a solution. That he'd find a way to help me stay with Charlie. I'd resisted his help every step of the way, but I'd take it now, willingly, if he had a way out of this mess.

"He's a kid. He's tougher and more malleable than you think. Now he's stronger than he'd ever have been. He'll grow up with a pack, and this will feel normal to him. This is the best place for Charlie to be and the worst place for you. I'll bring him to visit, or you might be able to visit here."

He turned his head, looking at the door, the counter, anywhere but me. My last hope was sinking fast.

There was an obvious out, and yet he said nothing about it. I was too desperate to remain quiet.

"Why can't we leave *with* Charlie? He's part of your pack. You were going to set up a separate place for your people anyway. Why can't you do it now? Would it be so bad to do it sooner? Then I can stay with him, and Charlie will still have shifters."

He still wasn't looking at me as he moved farther away. "I can't. I'm not going to be moving the pack somewhere else."

"What do you mean? Are you saying never? I don't understand." I got to my feet, tracing his steps across the room, afraid he'd run out on me before I got answers.

He finally looked at me, a hardness in his eyes. "We're merging the packs. We've been discussing it. It's better for all involved."

Better for all of them, but what had gone from a temporary separation from Charlie had just become years and years. It might as well be permanent. Charlie would grow up without me.

I reached out, gripping the counter for support. Duncan hated Groza, and now he was in essence saying he was going to mate with her? I stared at him, feeling like I didn't even know who he was.

"You just kissed me yesterday. Were you basically engaged to her then?" How could this be? What kind of evil person was he?

"Don't look at me like that. My arrangement with Groza is a business decision. We both made the choices we thought were best." He looked at the door, as if he wanted to get away from this entire discussion.

"How could you have kissed me, not once but twice, and not said a thing? How could you have let me agree to leave when it meant forever?" I'd never felt quite so betrayed by anyone in my life. My day had gone from horrible to the worst I might ever have.

"It's not like you had another choice," he said. "I wasn't looking for you to be forced out."

"You didn't walk away from the opportunity when it was in front of you, though, did you? Did you plan it with her? Wanting a pathetic little human must've been hard on your big alpha ego."

Even now, he was looking at my lips, and I'd never stepped away when he'd looked at me that way in the past. Well, there'd be plenty of steps in between us soon. Asking him had been a long shot, but I couldn't stop the pain at hearing the final nail in the coffin getting hammered in. How wrong I'd been about him.

I turned, needing to get back to Charlie and away from Duncan.

He stepped in my way. "I'm telling you, I didn't want this."

"I need to go. I don't want to waste my last few moments with you when they need to be spent with my brother."

He reached out, and his hand grazed my arm. I jerked it away and stepped around him.

"I'm sorry," he said.

I didn't respond.

Chapter Thirty-Two

I'D BEEN SITTING on Charlie's bed for an hour, watching him play with his train, wondering if I could somehow sneak him away. It was the wrong thing to do, but that didn't make it any easier to leave him here. He looked up at me and smiled, and it felt like someone was ripping my insides apart.

"Can we have Duncan's pancakes for lunch?" he asked. "I'm really hungry."

"I'm sure Duncan will make them for you, but I have to talk to you first. I have to tell you something that is very important." My voice was already cracking. How was I going to leave when I couldn't get through this conversation?

I took a deep breath, trying to hide my shuddering. "This might make you sad, but I want you to know it won't be forever."

"What?" There was already fear growing in his eyes.

"Well, because you're going to be able to shift, you're going to need to be with Duncan and the guys so they can teach you what you'll need to know. That's a very important thing for a shifter. But I won't be able to stay here with you while you learn."

"You're leaving?" His bottom lip quivered.

"I can't stay *here* because I don't shift, and this is a place for shifters. I won't be that far. I'll still see you. I'm going to tell Duncan and Buddie to bring you to visit me all the time."

He launched himself at me, wrapping his arms around my waist. "No. You said you wouldn't leave me. I want to go with you. I don't want to stay. I won't be a shifter, then."

I hugged him, forcing myself not to cry. I didn't want him to remember me falling apart. He couldn't know how bad this was, that it was the worst thing imaginable to me, only trumped by his dying. This was going to be okay. I'd make it okay somehow.

"I won't be far, and the time is going to fly by. Soon you'll be big enough to make your own choices and do whatever you want."

"No," he cried, hugging me tighter.

"Piper?" Duncan was at the door, looking at me.

I nodded, giving him the okay to intrude. I didn't want to give away the few minutes I had left, but if there was a chance Duncan could help, I'd take it, no matter how I felt about him at the moment.

"Charlie, I know your sister told you she was going to be leaving, but she's not going to be far," he said. "I can take you there whenever you want to see her."

"I don't want to visit. I want to go with her." Charlie lifted his head to stare at Duncan like he didn't understand a thing. I knew exactly how he felt.

"I know," Duncan said. "She doesn't want to leave you

either, but she has to. You know when you go to school and you have to follow rules? There are rules here too that people who can't shift can't stay that long. I'll be here for you whenever you need me. So will Buddie and the other guys."

Duncan rubbed his back, and I wanted to throw his hand off. I couldn't because Charlie needed this, but that was the only thing that stopped me.

Charlie didn't stop crying or let go. I wasn't sure how I was going to leave. Except I had no choice. If I didn't, Groza would have me killed. The kid was already going to have enough bad memories without adding that to the list.

I hugged him hard, as if I could somehow take him into my soul and protect him. I hugged him like I'd never see him again. Leaving him felt akin to someone putting my heart through a meat grinder. Only the hope that I'd somehow be able to get back to him one day, that I'd see him again, gave me the strength to go on.

"I have to go." I stood, losing the fight with my composure. If I didn't get out of here soon, Charlie would see me completely fall apart. I couldn't leave him with that memory. "I promise it's going to be okay," I said, trying to take a step away from him. "Come on, you can walk me out, okay?" He didn't answer, so I picked him up and carried him downstairs.

Buddie was walking in as I got to the door.

"Are you…" He took in the whole scene and then went mute.

I nodded.

"Buddie, can you take Charlie?" Duncan asked.

Buddie looked at me, as if afraid to try. I nodded. He reached for Charlie, who screamed and fought for a minute and then hugged Buddie, crying in his arms.

My whole body was shaking as I fought to hold it together. I grabbed my pack by the door and walked out before I lost it too.

Duncan followed me. "Give me a minute to grab my stuff."

I spun around. "I'll be fine. You don't need to worry about me."

"I want to go with you and see you settled."

"And I don't want you to." I hoped he could read the hatred in the glare I aimed at him.

His body went rigid as we stared. I wasn't bending on this. If I was leaving, I'd do it alone. Screw him *and* this place. Screw it all.

He must've read me enough to know it would be a knock-down, drag-out fight if he tried to come.

He nodded, rocking back on his heels for a minute. "I put a map and a compass in your pack. If you head south, it's two days' travel from here on foot. Stay near the river."

I didn't care about directions. Nothing mattered but Charlie.

"If something happens to him, I will kill you," I said.

"I'll take care of him. He's part of my pack now. Even more so, I'm the one who turned him. That creates a bond that I can't turn away from."

I nodded and turned to leave.

"At least let me walk—"

"No," I snapped. "I have to leave, and I'm done talking, especially to you." I was mad at the world right now, and he'd given me more ammo than most. The only silver lining about my leaving was getting away from him.

Groza watched me as I walked out. I would've killed her if I could've, and I wasn't taking anything off the table for the future. The other shifters looked on as well. Maybe I'd come back like Carrie at the prom one day and light them all on fire.

I walked out of the gates, each step away from Charlie like a razor slicing into me. I made it out of the place without shedding a tear in public but then cried for the next three hours. I stopped earlier than I'd planned, setting up my tent but forgoing a fire. I sat there until the sun went down.

I woke up at dawn the next morning and just lay there. I didn't care if it took me a month to get to this settlement. I might need that time in order to not break down into hysterics at even the mention of children.

At one point, there was a stirring nearby, but I still didn't rise. I didn't care if it was a bear about to maul me. I'd left Charlie. I'd done it to save him, but I'd left him nonetheless. I'd promised not to and I had. I should've negotiated harder. I should've figured out something to hold over Groza's head, some equal leverage. I hadn't. Now I'd left, and it felt like nothing in the world mattered.

Sometime around noon, I packed up my camp, checked the compass and the map, and started walking again. I meandered along the river, following the path I'd been told would lead me to the new settlement. I wasn't sure how far I'd gotten before I quit again for the night.

I settled beside a huge old tree and sat there. I ate a protein bar for dinner and a few swigs of water. A few hours later I opened up my bag and settled into it, not bothering with the tent, feeling like I was in a black hole of despair, with no way out. This felt worse than right after Death Day.

After the world ended, I hadn't had time to fall apart. I'd had to take care of Charlie. Now all I could think of was him, sad, scared, and disappointed in me for breaking my promise. I wasn't sure how I was going to go on. People say time heals all wounds, but this felt like a lethal blow that there'd be no coming back from. How could time heal anything when I felt like seconds were hours?

The last of the sun's rays faded as I lay there, wondering how I'd make it through the next day, let alone years.

Chapter Thirty-Three

THERE WERE footsteps in the dark, too close to run from, not that I had the urge. Someone had seen me. I hadn't been careful. I hadn't cared enough to bother.

I continued to feign sleep. The only hope now was that they'd take my things and leave me be. It was too risky to try to fight them off, and I didn't have the urge to fight anyway

Steps grew closer until I heard them right beside me.

"I know you're awake," Duncan said.

"What are you doing here?" I asked, sitting up, trying to wrap my head around his having followed me. Rage boiled up. "I told you I didn't need an escort, especially not you."

I'd been kicked out of the pack, not that I'd ever really been in it, and he was still trying to control my life. Well, he hadn't done that good of a job, because I no longer had Charlie, and Duncan couldn't call the shots anymore.

He knelt beside me. "I wasn't. Buddie was. But I came because I need to know what you talked to Jaysa about before she died."

"I'm done talking to you. Go away." I'd been banished

from the community, told I had to get out of the territory with implied threats of death, while he did nothing. I'd lost Charlie, and now he thought he was entitled to ask me something? Anything? In my book, he wasn't allowed to speak to me.

"I know you're angry, but—"

"But what? Groza needs me for something? You on an errand for your mate? Go. Away."

His chest expanded as he took a deep breath. "Are you incapable of having a civil discussion with me?"

"After what happened? Yes. I believe I am." I scooted off my sleeping bag and began to roll it up. If he wouldn't leave, then I would.

"Even if it means you might be able to come back?"

Might. He was dangling a carrot in front of a starving person, but I wasn't playing the game. I was done listening to him, speaking to him, acknowledging he was alive. I tied my roll to my pack and threw my bag over my shoulder.

He grabbed my arm, pulling me back to him when I tried to walk away.

"Get off me." I swatted at him.

"I'm not letting you leave without hearing me out. You might be able to come back and be with Charlie."

He was speaking as if I couldn't comprehend his words. I could. But I no longer believed what came out of his mouth.

"For what? A week while I do something else you need a lowly human for? Don't talk to me about coming back." It was hard to breathe when I thought of Charlie. Even hearing his name felt like an evisceration.

"You need to listen to me. It could potentially change everything." He was holding my shoulders, refusing to let me walk away.

"What do you want? Just say it and let me be," I screamed at him.

He leaned close, something almost frantic in his gaze. "I need to know what Jaysa said to you. I know she called for you the day before she died. I think she might have given you something."

"She didn't give me anything." I tried to shrug out of his grip again, but there was no budging him.

"Just tell me what she said."

I wanted to tell him to fuck off, then kick him in the balls and walk away like he couldn't hurt me anymore. But there were a couple glaring issues with that. One, he had Charlie. Two, it was him, and no matter how I'd like to pretend otherwise, I was drawn to him like I'd never been to another person in my life. The only other person who had entered my mind in the last two days was him, even as I cursed the day I met him. There was only one course of action: tell him what he wanted so he'd leave me be.

"If she gave me anything, it was a curse. I haven't felt right since the day she died." The stiffness had gotten moderately better, but I'd been plagued with fatigue—though that could be from the utter depression. It was hard to tell.

I yanked my arms harder, forcing him to either fight me or let me go. Was it a nice gesture? I didn't know or care. Everything made me angry. His possibly watching me from afar as I'd wallowed stabbed at my open wound.

"She didn't give me anything. I don't need you or your people, so just *go*."

He finally let go of my shoulders, but it was to grab my hand. "You're wrong. I think I can feel it. I don't know why she chose you, but she did, and it's something the pack needs."

"I don't know if you're having a breakdown from guilt or remorse or whatever, but it's done, so you need to leave."

"Not until we try something. You do this and it doesn't work, I'll leave you alone."

"Oh, so now I need to come back because it benefits *you*?" If I could've beaten him at that moment, I would've. I didn't think my hate could grow stronger than it was right now.

"If you don't want to come back, I get it. I wouldn't like us either if I were you. I'd probably do the exact same thing—but you want to be with Charlie. If I'm right, they'll accept you because of it, or at least not try to hurt you. Groza will have to accept you too. It's up to you." He kept looking at me as if I wasn't understanding.

I understood too well. That was the problem. I didn't trust him at all. I trusted none of them. The thing my heart couldn't get past was walking away from Charlie if there was the smallest chance at fixing this.

I swallowed my hate back only long enough to hear him out. "What exactly is it you think she gave me?"

"Her gift."

He knelt down, brushing away at the ground until the leaves and sticks were pushed away and there was a hole of dark, rich earth.

"Put your hands into the dirt and leave them there until I tell you to pull them out."

The whole thing seemed ridiculous, but I knelt down in front of his cleared spot.

I glanced up at him after a minute or so. "Are we waiting for something? You want me to just stay like this all night?"

"Our kind, our abilities—our magic, if you will, it comes from the Earth, from nature. If she did what I think, what she gave you has never been given to a human before. It might take a while to transfer."

"And this is how I'm going to get fixed? Sticking my hands in some dirt?"

"It's sort of a parlor trick, but yes—it won't do it all, but it'll help."

"Why do you think she gave me anything?" I shifted, realizing I should've gotten into a more comfortable position if I was going to be sitting here with my hands shoved in the dirt for a while.

"Because we've been waiting for signs to show up in someone else, and nothing has. Then as soon as you left, the well dried up overnight, the cows went dry, and half the crop died."

I looked up at him, even though it gave me a crick in my neck in my current position. "That's why you think it's me? You didn't happen to notice the drought going on?"

I moved to pull my hands out, but he grabbed my wrists to hold them in the dirt.

His eyes went to where he was holding me. "You don't feel that?"

"Feel what? Dirt? Couple worms slithering around?"

He kept his hands wrapped around my wrists, and there was a light in his eyes as he looked at me. "Maybe you can't feel it since you're generating it, but I can."

He let go of my wrists and stood. "This changes everything. You not only can come back, but the pack *needs* you."

"I don't care what the pack needs," I said, getting to my feet and brushing off my hands.

"But you care about Charlie," he said, knowing he had the winning hand.

"If I go back, he sees me, and then I have to leave again—"

"You won't. I'll give you my word." He stepped closer to me. This time I took a step back. I'd never let him get near me again, not like that.

"What if Groza rejects me anyway? Says I have to go?" I didn't doubt she would.

"You're the new guide. That's it. The pack will revolt against her before they let her drive you out. She has no choice in this."

Then nothing else mattered. Not my hatred of Duncan, Groza, any of them. If I could go back for Charlie, I was going.

"What do I do?"

He wanted to smile. He was happy, and it made me hate him more. Did he enjoy how my life was getting jerked around?

"This isn't for you or the pack," I said.

That took some of the edge off the joy I saw, and I was glad I'd hurt him.

"We need to get you putting out enough of a charge that when we go back into the pack tomorrow, they can feel it too."

"Fine. What should I do?"

"Have you ever seen kids bury people on the beach? I need to do that to you here."

"You want to bury me in dirt?" The man had gone crazy.

"Just for tonight. I'm hoping it'll help you transition enough that they can feel it too. And if they do, there is no way Groza can make you leave."

"Start digging."

———

I woke with the sunrise, and instead of feeling like the walking dead, not even sure how I'd rise, I felt like I was among the living again. It was the best I'd felt in days.

"You don't have to tell me. I can see it. More importantly, I can feel it," Duncan said. He offered me a hand to help me up.

I ignored it, pushing and shoving at the dirt, crawling my way out of the ground. It made me wonder if this was how a zombie felt digging its way out of the grave. What kind of creature I might turn into was a mystery, but right now I was filthy and in need of a shower. I went to the river to clean the dirt from me.

He'd cleaned up the camp by the time I got back.

"You ready to go home?" he asked.

"I'm ready to go back to Charlie." The settlement wasn't my home. I wasn't wanted there, but they needed my woo-woo magic, or what they thought I had, so they'd tolerate me.

He nodded, not taking the bait.

I grabbed my pack from his hand before he could put it on.

"I'll carry my own things."

He nodded, again, not fighting with me.

"I won't be staying in the cottage with you either."

"That's fine. I'll be expected to move in with Groza anyway."

I put my chin up, as if that were acceptable, even as it burned. What else could I expect? They were mated, right? That was how things would be.

We walked back, and I shut down all the conversations he tried to start. We neared the settlement by that night. Getting back to Charlie had put an urgency in my strides that was missing when I left.

The rain was coming down by the time we were outside the community.

I paused for a minute, shooting Duncan a look.

"I promise," he said.

He'd better stand by his word, or I would kill him. I wasn't leaving again. Or, at least, I wasn't leaving again without my brother.

By the time we were standing on the main thoroughfare, it was pouring. More than a few people were standing on their porches. I could see them watching me with curiosity.

"Well? Now what?" I asked.

"Just stand there and wait," he said.

I stood there as requested, feeling ridiculous and like a fraud. Had Duncan really even felt anything? How had I believed him? I was standing in the rain, not moving, like an idiot. That was why they were staring.

Slowly, a couple people walked over, squinting, as if not believing what they saw.

One of the younger women hesitantly reached forward. Her fingers were nearly trembling as they got closer. She laid a hand on me. Her lips parted on a gasp as she looked up.

"It's true! It's her!"

Another person reached a tentative hand out, touching me. They yanked it back, gasping. Then another did. There were some shouts as more people gathered around. Soon they were all coming out of their homes and buildings, standing around me, looking at me, almost in reverence.

I'd bent over backward to try to get along, and all I had to do was bury myself in some dirt and stand in the rain?

Groza appeared on the outskirts of the crowd that had gathered, glaring at me. No one so much as glanced her way. I wasn't sure they noticed her there while I waited for her to push her way through the crowd and demand I leave.

She didn't. She stood staring for five minutes or so and

then turned on her heel, looking as unhappy as I'd ever seen her. I might've won this battle, but there was going to be a long war ahead of me if I stayed. Which meant I better get ready for war, because I wasn't leaving again.

Charlie darted this way and that through the crowd. I saw the joy on his face as he ran toward me and flung himself into my arms the moment he got close. He wrapped his arms around my neck like he'd never let go again, and I could already feel how much stronger he'd gotten just in the last couple of days.

"You came back," he said, squeezing my neck so tight that I was afraid he'd cut off my air.

"Yes. I'm not leaving, either."

I was suddenly glad for the rain so it could hide the streaming tears.

Charlie pulled back after a few more minutes. "Why do you feel weird?"

He felt it too? Was it possible that Duncan was right? That all these people were too? Had Jaysa transferred something to me?

"I'm not sure. But we'll figure it out."

With Charlie still in my arms, I turned and headed in the direction of the cottage before they changed their minds and tried to make me leave again. The group followed me, trailing at a distance. They were staring as if stunned.

Chapter Thirty-Four

I WAS SITTING on one of the new rocking chairs on the porch. Buddie had brought them over this morning and declared them a homecoming present.

I couldn't remember when I told him I'd always wanted a porch like this with rocking chairs, but he'd remembered.

He watched me as he sipped his coffee and Charlie played with a couple of kids in the yard.

"Interesting day yesterday, huh?" Buddie said.

I'd been waiting for him to broach the topic for the last half an hour. "Yeah, you could say that."

"How are you feeling?"

"Actually a bit better today. Maybe more settled in my body, if that makes sense." I wasn't even sure if it made sense to *me*, but it was the best answer I could come up with. I wasn't sure what would become of me, but I'd deal with it as it came.

Charlie looked over at the porch for the tenth time, reassuring himself that I was still there. It would take him a while to feel more secure, but he would. It might take a little longer to trust everything I said, but that would come too.

"Crazy how things work out," Buddie said. "Jaysa gave you her gift. No one thought it could transfer to a human, but it did. Maybe it could always transfer, or maybe there's something about you that made it possible. Point is, it happened."

"What does that mean to me in the simplest terms? What am I going to become?" I said.

"I don't know. I'm not sure how it'll manifest in you, but I know it's happening. Now we wait and see."

"What if I don't want to be this thing? What if I don't want to be in the pack at some point?" Was this a life sentence? Now that I had a quiet moment to think, the questions wouldn't stop coming.

"You can try to leave, but they won't let you," Buddie said, and laughed.

"They?"

He waved a hand at the people walking down the streets. "Yes. Your leaving puts their lives in jeopardy. As eager as they were to kill you before? They'll fight to *keep* you now."

I spotted Duncan walking down the other end of the street with Groza. He looked my way. I stared back, hoping he could see me well enough to read the anger in my eyes. I might be back here, but that didn't change anything between us.

Groza grabbed his arm, attempting to pull his attention back to her. I saw him turn, and it looked as if they were having words. Already trouble in paradise, I guess. No less than he deserved.

Buddie let out a low whistle. "I can see how pissed off you are, but you're reading this wrong."

"Really? I don't know about that. I'm not sure someone

who's engaged should be actively kissing other people. That one is pretty obvious."

"That's assuming he was engaged when he kissed you," Buddie said, sounding a bit put out.

I turned and stared at him. "Wasn't he?"

"First I heard of them mating and joining the packs was after they transitioned Charlie."

I stopped rocking. "Are you saying... You can't mean..."

He looked at me, as if how could I not see it. "He didn't do it for him, that's for sure. He can't stand Groza. Never could."

"Are you saying he did this for me? For Charlie?" I felt a huge crack forming in my wall of hate. It couldn't be true, could it?

"Certainly seems that way, doesn't it? He gave Groza what she's been after for years, or so she thinks. I still don't think she actually is going to get what she wants." He got up and walked closer. "I wouldn't let your guard down, though. Mark my words—this won't be the end of it with her."

That wouldn't be a problem. The days of being carefree were gone.

A couple months ago, the world had been different. People had been softer, kinder, more generous, or I'd thought they were. I was wondering if any of that had been true. If it was, how could so many of them turn into the people they were now? Perhaps the saying that only the good die young was true, because the people left living were savages. It didn't really matter, though, only in so much that the world we currently lived in bore no resemblance to what life used to be. If I wanted to survive, I needed to be more brutal than the people I walked amongst.

I might not be the toughest yet, but I was working on it. I wasn't just going to survive this world, but thrive in it.

. . .

Look for book two of Life After Death Day early next year.

scan the QR code to join my mailing list.

Follow me on one of these platforms:
https://www.facebook.com/groups/223180598486878/
http://www.donnaaugustine.com
https://www.bookbub.com/authors/donna-augustine
https://twitter.com/DonnAugustine

Acknowledgments

I don't believe any book can every read its full potential without fresh eyes. I'm lucky to have quite a few pairs that are willing to pitch in. Donna Z., Ashley M., Lori K., Lisa A., Camilla J. and Karen C, each one of you helped this book get across the finish line, and I'm forever grateful!

Also by Donna Augustine

The Wilds

The Wilds

The Hunt

The Dead

The Magic

Born Wild (Wilds Spinoff)

Wild One

Savage One

Ollie Wit

A Step into the Dark

Walking in the Dark

Kissed by the Dark

Going Nowhere

A Bridge to Nowhereland

Burning Bridges in Nowhere

Out of Nowhere

The Keepers

The Keepers

Keepers and Killers

Shattered

Redemption

Karma

Karma

Jinxed

Fated

Dead Ink

Wyrd Blood

Wyrd Blood

Full Blood

Blood Binds

Torn Worlds (Paranormal Romance)

Gut Deep

Visceral Reaction

River of Luck

Made in the USA
Coppell, TX
01 December 2023

25092488R00153